Journey of Light: Trilogy

By

Stewart Bitkoff, Ed. D.

authorHOUSE

1663 LIBERTY DRIVE, SUITE 200
BLOOMINGTON, INDIANA 47403
(800) 839-8640
www.authorhouse.com

First published by AuthorHouse 05/17/04

ISBN: 1-4184-0258-3 (e)
ISBN: 1-4184-0256-7 (sc)

This book is printed on acid-free paper.

*In order to affect a work there must be
the coming together of multiple factors.*

*Also, there must be an alignment
of the right people at the right time
and in the right place.*

*Many thanks to Melody, Holly, and Leola
for helping bring forward this collection
and mixing the stew.*

*Love
SB*

Table of Contents

INTRODUCTION   IX

IN THE BOOKSELLER'S HAND   2

    I - The Emergency Room   3

    II - Graduate Study   5

    III - Troubled Sleep   7

    IV - The Lightbearer   9

    V - The Confrontation   11

    VI - A Telephone Call   13

    VII – Amoun   15

    VIII - Continuing the Discussion   17

    IX - Brothers & Sisters   21

    X - Dr. Lannis   23

    XI - A Lesson   25

    XII - Why Are You Here?   27

    XIII - A Walk in the Park   29

    XIV - Submission   31

    XV - The Teacher's Job   33

XVI - Journal Entry   39

XVII - The Path   41

XVIII - A Suggestion   45

XIX - Dr. Lannis' Office   47

XX - Lessons   51

XXI - Searching for Amoun   55

XXII - Getting Closer   59

XXIII - The Rainbow Body   61

XXIV - I Remember   65

TEDDY'S LAST SWIM IN PARADISE LAND   68

I – Introduction   69

II – Scott   73

III – Helen   89

IV – Sarah   97

V - Paradise Land   111

VI – Happiness   119

VII – Moving On   123

THE JUDGMENT OF JULIE

THE JUDGMENT OF JULIE 126

I – Introduction 129

II - Simkus Family Tree 131

III - The Apartment on Union Avenue 133

IV - An Enriching Element 161

V - Three Events 171

VI - The Judgment 181

Introduction

The message has always been the same. We are the ones who have forgotten. The religion is one and humanity has a common source. Over time, messengers and religious forms vary. This confuses people.

The Light is the binding force of the universe and is the mother and father of us all. It is the great river from which we all came. On the surface, the river's water shifts due to changing currents and wind. Yet, beneath the surface the water remains calm and tranquil.

In this age, people are frightened and searching for something to help ease their fear and unite them. It is there, but we have forgotten to go deep and embrace our common spiritual heritage.

Within each, the Light is waiting to bring us home and illume the darkness.

Journey of Light: Trilogy presents three tales of spiritual awakening. Each tells the story of how a man came to embrace the Light.

In the Bookseller's Hand is based upon actual events and recounts a young man's encounter with a spiritual Master. On the first night of graduate school, the protagonist realizes that there is another kind of learning awaiting him on the streets of Manhattan. It is here, in a mysterious bookstore, he meets someone who challenges his worldview and the inner journey begins.

Teddy's Last Swim in Paradise Land follows Teddy Polinski as he travels from psychiatric hospital to nursing home and visits his son and wife. Caring for those he loves has worn Teddy out and he is nearing a breaking point. Yet, somewhere in Teddy's past is a 'ladder' to help him climb the fence he has built around himself. Teddy must journey back to Paradise Land to recover what he lost.

The Judgment of Julie opens on the day of Julie Simkus' death. Julie awakens on the other side and finds himself going over events of his life. He relives moments when he hurt others and fell short of the mark. Through this self-examination, Julie learns what is lasting and begins the journey home.

Finally, to those who are concerned about the accuracy of events, characters and failed behavior, literary license was taken.

While characters and events are based upon actual people, some facts were altered to serve the story line. With respect to flaws, individuals are every man with multiple strengths and weaknesses. To those who find this objectionable to someone's memory, my apology. The intent of doing this was to make specific ideas and teachings accessible to the reader.

Book 1

In the Bookseller's Hand

****

The student questioned, "Master, why don't more of the people take what you offer them? In your hand you hold a wondrous element that can transform their lives."

The Master replied, "I extend my hand to everyone, yet few see what I hold. Most never open their eyes."

"Then why don't you teach them to open their eyes," inquired the student.

"First, they must be willing and able to learn," replied the Master.

****

I - The Emergency Room

The doctors say I need to rest, having suffered a shock of some kind. They claim I should talk about what happened, let it out, and then I will be free of it. I am reluctant to do this. If I tell the story, they will surely put me away. In fact, that was what the doctors first discussed when I was found by the Police, wandering the streets mumbling, "Amoun, Amoun."

In the emergency room, I overheard Dr. Lannis talking with Dr. Cohen. Cohen whispered to Lannis, "loss of memory brought on by trauma or drugs. We will have to wait for the lab results, but my instincts say shock brought on by trauma. Clearly, temporary loss of awareness due to a violent event.

"The next few hours and how he responds to our questions will determine if we can release him. Minimally, he will require medication and psychiatric follow-up for two months. Then, depending upon how he progresses, he can return to normal duties whatever those might be. Have the nurses contacted his wife? She should have been here by now. Perhaps she can help us figure out what happened?"

Little did the doctors realize my wife could not help. Lea had no idea what happened; it was a mystery to her as well. She remembered me saying that I needed to go to the library and work on a research paper for school. That was Saturday. Today is Friday. She has not heard from me in six days.

Over that time, Lea was frantic and feared the worst. The secretary at work called on Monday, wondering if I was sick, and indicated it was so unlike me not to call.

By Sunday evening, after dozens of phone calls and not finding me, Lea put the Police to work by filing a missing person's report. At first, the Police told Lea not to worry, that I was probably out with a girlfriend and would be home in a couple of days. The Police questioned Lea about our marriage and my daily habits, including drug and alcohol history. These things I learned over the past few days. Now that I am back home, Lea is more relaxed though I can still

3

hear her crying sometimes. Daily she asks me what happened and encourages me to talk about it, just like the doctors said.

It has been two weeks since the Police brought me to the emergency room. Slowly, the events are coming back and I am starting to make sense out of it all. The doctors were right in assuming I have suffered a shock and I am trying to work out the sequence of events by writing down what happened. If I talk about it with anyone, I am afraid they will lock me away.

The medicine the doctors gave me for my nerves does not work; it just makes me drowsy and I fall asleep. I do not want to sleep. I want to remember and stay awake. Most of my life I have been walking in a daze and it has taken a shock for me to finally realize it.

As the days pass, I realize I have been changed and can never go back to the way I was. It is time for something else to happen; it is time for another part of me to come forward. Oh, I will work, be a loving husband and be part of the world, but I will always look at things a little differently. Now, I have a broader perspective; a spiritual way of looking at things. The dirt covering my glasses has been removed.

Someday, I will share what happened with Lea and talk to her about it. Now, it is still too much of a jumble. I can not tell the doctors, for as scientists they will never understand. When I finish writing and sorting out the pieces, it will be time to share what happened and move on. A whole new life awaits Lea and I.

This is how I came to awake from this slumber called life and understand more fully my place in the universe.

II - Graduate Study

Intentionally, I arrived early for the first day of graduate school, wanting to walk around the city and college campus soaking up the atmosphere. I rode the Subway to 14th street and walked down Broadway toward Washington Square Park and New York University (NYU). Besides enjoying the activity of the city streets, I wanted to visit a few bookstores before class.

This was an exciting time for me. I was newly married, worked full-time, and had been accepted into a doctoral program. I had everything I needed out of life and wanted only to enjoy the moments before class.

The city was alive with colors, busy people and endless smells. It was early autumn and there was a faint chill to the air. As I gazed into the different store windows that lined Broadway, I felt alive and grateful to be working toward one of my dreams.

I was beginning doctoral study at one of the finest universities in the land. Tonight began my ascent toward higher learning. All those years of preparation were necessary for this moment when the gates of academia would open and embrace me. I was one of the chosen and soon would be given access to knowledge.

As I write this, I have to laugh at how naïve this all sounds. However, it is true; I actually thought doctoral preparation was the pinnacle of learning. Over the ensuing weeks, I learned there was another type of learning and with it knowledge that rivaled, and even exceeded, what was taught behind university walls.

Slowly I made my way down toward NYU and came upon another bookstore. I had already browsed two others hungrily wanting to consume all the knowledge around me. This bookstore was different than the others; it specialized in occult, metaphysical and religious books. In fact, it was the largest bookstore of its kind in New York City and a veritable supermarket of exotic writing. Each aisle held a different selection of spiritual and metaphysical thought. As I wandered about these books, I thought to myself, someday, after completing my doctorate, I needed to make a study of this material as well. Surely there was something in religion that called to me but first I had to study the knowledge of the world and university.

As I made my way from between the aisles and toward the front of the store, I saw him. He was standing behind the counter, next to the young woman who worked the cash register. An elderly man with gray hair, olive complexion and a warm smile. He was standing with his back towards the books and, as I walked past him, he looked directly into my eyes and extended his right hand out, palm-up. Continuing on, I looked at his extended hand and shook my head, "No," thinking he was asking for a handout, a donation for the store. What nerve, I thought, crossing the street to make my way toward the Main Building, not wanting to be late for my first class.

III - Troubled Sleep

That evening, arriving home at 9 p.m., I found Lea waiting to hear about graduate school and the first day of class. Enthusiastically, I described the city, the university and my different classmates. My class was on the theory of education and college preparation. Students ranged from college professors to superintendents of schools from local suburban school districts. For me, it was a thrill to be amongst them and share the learning experience.

Later, after the excitement wore off, I had trouble falling asleep. This was very unusual. Usually as soon as I hit the pillow, I was out. Most of the time, I slept the sleep of the innocent and clear of conscience.

Not that night, as something disturbed me and kept me awake. All kinds of thoughts raced through my head. At first, I thought the trouble sleeping was due to the lingering excitement of the day and starting a new phase in my life. Over time, I realized how deep the discontentment was and what triggered its rise to the surface.

About 3 a.m., though unsettled, I finally fell asleep. Upon awakening at 6:30 for work, I was tired and drained feeling like I had struggled through the night.

IV - The Lightbearer

I remember that the day at work was busy, there being many patients at the hospital who needed therapy. Our recreation programs were filled and time went quickly.

When I got home from work, I had dinner, read for class and finally called it a night about 9 p.m. Lea and I watched some television until 11 o'clock when we both got sleepy and went to bed.

Again, I had trouble falling asleep. I tossed and turned until 1 a.m. So that I would not wake Lea, I got-up, went out into the living room and lay down on the sofa. After lots of racing thoughts, I finally dozed off.

Sometime during the night, I became aware of what was bothering me. In that middle place, between sleep and consciousness, I saw him again. In my dream, the old man from the bookstore was smiling at me he held his right hand out and whispered, "Why don't you take what I am offering you?"

Then, I heard myself reply, "What are you offering? I don't see anything. You just want money."

Again he whispered, "Look closer." As I focused harder, slowly, I began to see a luminous round shape take form in his hand. Gradually, it grew brighter and more intense; suddenly, it was a glimmering, pulsating ball of white Light resting just above his hand. With each second, the Light grew stronger and brighter. Then, the orb was aglow with a peaceful, calming energy that called to me on a deep, inner level.

The old man smiled again and whispered, "Now you see it and are forever changed. Your slumber has ended." With that said, the old man was gone, but the peacefulness of the Light stayed with me and I felt its warm, loving rays as I slept.

When I awoke to the ringing of the alarm at 6:30 a.m., I was refreshed and had forgotten all about the old man and the dream. In fact, I thought nothing about the dream until much later that evening when I again had trouble sleeping. At 1 a.m., I found myself back on the sofa dozing off. Again, I was awakened in my dream by the old man holding his hand out and whispering, "Why do you refuse what I offer you?" This time, I could see nothing in his hand.

Over the next few nights, I had the same dream. Each evening, the old man beckoned to me with extended hand, whispering, "Why don't you take what I am offering you?" Unable to see the white, peaceful orb, I awoke anxious. I missed the peaceful, calming energy that the Light gave off and wanted more of it.

As I worked each day, studied in the early evening and had family responsibilities, there was not much time to think about the old man. When he did enter my mind, I thought, had the old bookseller put a spell on me? I wondered what sort of magic he worked and why I had been susceptible. There had always been unrest inside of me. Perhaps, the old man felt it and was using it for a sinister purpose? Or, maybe I made the whole thing up? Was I losing my mind? Was I working too hard?

These questions filled my mind and the range of possible answers did not ease my concern. At the time, I did not know what it was, but something else was going on. I had changed inside. Deep within, I was not the same. I was pre-occupied and could feel it. It all seemed to begin on the first day of graduate school; after I left the bookstore.

V - The Confrontation

On Tuesday afternoon, as I rode the Subway down to St. Mark's Place, my mind was not on the education theory class that began at 4 p.m. I was anxious and troubled, wondering what was going on. A week ago I was filled with anticipation about the new phase I had begun. Now, a few days later, this excitement was replaced with fear and anxiety. I felt as if the very fabric of my life had come undone.

At first, I had no intention of going back to the bookstore and confronting the old man. During the week, I thought about this confrontation several times. Yet, how do you accuse someone of entering your mind? The old man would just laugh and tell me to go see a psychiatrist.

Riding on the subway, I forced myself not to think about the old man, the bookstore or the recurring dream. I exerted my will and pushed the whole thing out of my mind. I considered an alternate explanation for the phenomenon. With the start of graduate study, I overworked myself and my mind fixed on this problem to divert anxiety about school. Clearly, I was worrying about the old man instead of concentrating on school. My mind created this defense mechanism.

As I rounded the corner of St. Mark's Place and Broadway, purposefully I crossed the street. The bookstore was down Broadway one block on the left and I wanted to be on the right side. I did not want to be tempted to look into the store just to see if I could catch a glimpse of the old man. At a brisk pace, I walked down Broadway wanting to get to class early. Passing the bookstore, I felt something stir inside of me; it was an inner acknowledgment and pull that called me to enter the store. Not to honor this call would be against my own higher nature and the laws of the universe.

I do not recall crossing the street or entering the bookstore. I remember asking the young woman who worked the cash register, "Where is the owner?"

I do not know how I knew the old man was the owner, I just did. Pointing toward the back of the store, she replied, "He is in the back office."

11

Without a glance, I walked past the books on Confucius, Magic, Witchcraft, Yoga, Zoroaster, Rumi, and a dozen other topics. Quickly I saw the office, walked up to the door and knocked. Then, I heard a soft voice say, "Come in." Hesitantly, I opened the door, stepped into the small room where the old man was seated behind a desk. He looked-up from some paperwork and smiled. Then whispered, "So you have come. I see you received my message."

Shaking my head in bewilderment, I replied, "What message?"

"The dream. Please, have a seat and I will explain."

VI - A Telephone Call

Lea announced, "Phone call. You have a call from Dr. Lannis."

I stopped writing and replied, "I'll get it." Picking up the phone in the study I said, "Hi, Dr. Lannis, how are you?"

Lannis replied, "Fine, but how are you? That's why I am calling, to find out how the patient is doing? Are things getting any clearer about those missing days?"

Pausing to consider my answer I said, "Bits and pieces are coming back."

"Good," said Lannis. "Let's make an appointment for next week to talk about it. How's Wednesday at 10 a.m.?"

"Fine," I said.

"Are you writing any of it down in your journal?"

Not wanting to lie, I replied, "Yes."

"Good. Very good. Then bring it with you."

"See you next Wednesday," I said and hung up the phone.

Boy, I hated shrinks! Working with them, I realized both how helpful and intrusive they could be. The best of them taught you how to figure out your own problems. That's just what I was doing when Lannis called; working out my own problems. Reading over what I had written, I realized that, unless I was real sure myself, it would be a stretch for Lannis to accept this story. Alternate uses of the mind was an area shrinks were just beginning to investigate themselves. As scientists, psychiatrists were at the frontier of the relationship between consciousness and reality.

With the clock now ticking, I suddenly realized the urgency of figuring out what happened before my next appointment. Once, I could have lied to Lannis or simply not have kept the appointment, but the time for evasiveness had passed. I had to be true to my own higher nature and understand what had happened.

Lea called out, "What did Lannis want?"

"He wants to see me and talk about what I have written in my journal," I said.

Lea replied, "Good. Keep writing."

VII – Amoun

I sat down on the folding chair in front of a gray metal desk. The office was stark except for the desk, two folding black chairs, an old brown file cabinet and a small wooden table behind the desk for coffee. Sitting behind the desk, the old man was exactly as he appeared in my dreams; gray hair, olive complexion, slight build, about 70 years of age, wearing a brown sweater and dark blue slacks.

From appearance there was nothing unusual about him; just your average senior citizen. If you met him in the grocery store, you would talk to him and like him. You might, even in time, become his friend; he had a trusting quality about him. Yet, something told me to be on guard. Somehow, he had worked his way into my mind.

"Would you like some coffee?" asked the old man.

"No," I said, afraid that there might be something inside it.

"Do you mind if I have some?"

"Help yourself."

Waiting as the old man turned and made his coffee, I wondered what the hell I was doing there. Class was to start in 10 minutes and I was in an office with an old man. Do I go out of my way to make problems for myself?

After the old man turned back around and sipped his coffee, he began. "Thank you for coming and replying to my message. My name is Amoun and this is my bookstore. The other day, when you were here and walked past me, I perceived the fragrance about you. That is what I called to."

I did not know what to say. What was he talking about? Trying not to be rude, I introduced myself and said, "Yes, I did stop in here last week just before class at the university. In fact, I am late for class now."

"I am sorry," said Amoun. "I did not mean to keep you from your duties. In fact, I have something you need and would like to discuss it with you at your convenience. Is this Saturday at 10 a.m. a better time? I will be here and we can have our discussion at a more leisurely pace."

"I really have to go…What do you have that I could possibly need?" I wondered aloud and stood turning toward the door.

Amoun extended out his right hand and whispered, "the Light."

Turning back I saw the small orb of glowing, shimmering, white Light suspended above his hand. Its peaceful energy called out and again entered deep inside of me. For a moment, I stood there transfixed. Then, I looked into Amoun's eyes and back at the white Light. They were both the same.

Befuddled, not knowing what to say, I stammered, "I have to leave now, I am late for class." I ran out of the office and heard behind me Amoun softly chuckling to himself.

I do not remember the rest of that evening, except arriving late for class and the loving peace of the white Light above Amoun's hand. Now, that seems a long time ago.

VIII - Continuing the Discussion

Of course, there would be nothing more to write about if I did not return that Saturday to Amoun's. All through the rest of the week, working at the hospital, studying and being with Lea, I thought only of the white Light. There was a peacefulness and knowing that emanated from the bookseller's hand that called to me. I knew that place. It was my home. Then, why did I run away? What was I frightened of? I had to have the answer and reconcile my fear.

"Would you like some coffee?" Amoun asked.

"Yes," I replied.

Amoun got up, poured some coffee into a cup and inquired, "Milk or sugar?"

"Black," I replied.

Amoun brought me the coffee, sat down behind his small desk and said, "How is the coffee?"

I took a sip. It was hot and strong. Just as I liked it. "Fine."

"Good, now let's get down to business. Why are you here?"

Somewhat surprised, I offered, "Because you invited me."

"No, that's not what I meant," said Amoun. "Why are you here in this realm? What is the purpose of your life? Where will you go after you leave?"

Not wanting a verbal duel I knew I could not win and not wanting to be rude to an elder, I replied, "I do not know." I really wanted to say, "why don't you just tell me…" But I kept my mouth shut.

Appearing as if he somehow heard that last thought, Amoun stared at me and said, "Not knowing is a good answer. Admitting lack of knowledge is a good start. Counter theories about the purpose of life, smart wise cracks and thinking one knows it all are not the correct posture. One must be cautious and open at the same time."

I wondered, had he read my mind?

Amoun looked at me with a twinkle in his eye and smiled.

What had I got myself into? I was frightened and pleaded, "Please, tell me what all of this is about. I am confused and worried.

17

These last two weeks I have been preoccupied, aware something has been missing from my life for a very long time. What is going on?"

"Deep within, there is an emptiness and yearning. This emptiness and yearning is the reason for all inquiry and learning. It is the reason for the journey and can only be filled by the Light. Throughout the ages, people have sought to fill this yearning and hunger with all kinds of things. Treasure, philosophy, religion, sex, drugs, power, fine position and wealth are but a few of the substitutes. They cannot fill the hunger and many have confused the object of the search.

"You have come because a part of you recognizes there is something here you need and must have. Like calls to like. You could not have stayed away. The Beloved Calls and you must reply…"

As Amoun continued talking I listened with my full attention. The words seemed to ring true. Yet, something else was happening in the room. There seemed to be an energy emanating from the old man; it reached out and touched a hidden part of me. Suddenly, I was alive and aglow with an inner awareness. I felt connected to the old man, the energy and everything in the room. The closest thing to this I ever felt was when I first met my wife and looked into her beautiful, blue eyes. Instantly, my heart awoke with love and I never wanted to leave her side.

This experience was similar, but different in degree. I was one with this energy and could not tell where I ended and it began. I recognized this energy and was content to stay in this place forever. We had all come from this energy and had forgotten.

Suddenly, I wondered, What was in the coffee Amoun gave me? Was there some kind of drug at work?

Angrily, I looked at Amoun and he smiled. Softly, he replied, "It is not the coffee. It is your own inner song. You have awakened from your slumber and recognized the Light as home. Ask me the questions that are in your heart."

Timidly, I began. "If the purpose of the journey is to find the Light, wouldn't it simplify things if we were born knowing this? So much effort, so much struggling could be avoided if we were born with this in our consciousness."

"The point of the journey is to come to the Light on your own; it is a matter of love and choice. Deep within there is a yearning and restlessness that can only be filled by the Light; this connection leads us on from realm to realm.

"Man is God's emissary and has within a wonderful capacity to love and create. This capacity is a magical wand and cannot be given, or awakened, without safeguards. The safeguards are part of the journey and this capacity has to be earned through free will and love.

"The Light is your home; it is the mother and father of us all. It is both the beginning and end. Each of us has within a spark from this wondrous element. It is this spark which the teacher re-kindles by reflecting the Light upon the student's heart. In time, through proper direction and love of the Light, this spark burns brighter, guiding the traveler. That is what you are feeling, stirring and coming aglow in your heart."

"If this is so simple, why do we complicate the journey with all manner of religions, philosophies, and beliefs?" I asked.

"Each time and place is different. The culture of the middle east, 2000 years ago is different than the culture of today. People's needs and understanding of things vary. Presentations are specific to time and place. Externally, the Light manifests in different colors. Internally, it is always the same. When the Light filters through a prism, it is changed into a beautiful spectrum of colors; yet, it is the same Light. Do you understand?"

I nodded my head in agreement, yet these words confirmed things I had always known. This business about one religion being the only true faith bothered me. How could the Creator love one group of people more than another? This never made sense. Yet, this is what some religions say to their followers. "We are correct and the others are mistaken. Also, it is our duty to convert and help spread the message."

While it is good to share belief with others, often I felt presentations coerced and threatened. Usually, the non-believer faced punishment. The God, or Light I hoped to worship was gentler and more loving. This Creator did not have to threaten to make a point.

By this time, I lost track of what was taking place. Somehow, my soul was transported; it had become alive with a loving, pulsating energy. I was connected to all things and no longer cared about questions. I was alive with the Light of eternity and found the answer. When you have found the answer you no longer require questions.

At this point, Amoun smiled and said, "our time is over. If you are free next Saturday, return at 10 a.m. and we will continue our talk. Incidentally, the caress the Beloved has bestowed will continue for about 24 hours. Enjoy your gift and give something to the poor in His Name."

With this instruction, I stood and shook Amoun's hand and smiled as I left the office.

In a daze, I walked toward the front of the store and felt the Light dancing about me. As I went past the cashier, the young woman questioned, "did you find what you were looking for?"

I looked at her, smiled and replied, "more than I ever imagined."

She looked into my eyes and said, "please come back."

Walking out the front door, something told me to look up at the sign over head. Realizing I walked past the store and been inside several times without noticing the store's name, I looked up. Lettered in gold and black paint was **Lightbearer Books**. The letters were set across a rising, yellow and orange sun. Continuing on toward the Subway, I thought, "what a perfect name."

IX - Brothers & Sisters

Riding home on the Subway north to the Bronx, I was filled with all kinds of thoughts, and feelings and awareness. The energy, which pulsated through me, was unlike anything I had ever known. It was like putting my finger inside an electrical outlet, only there was no pain just electricity. The Light awakened my inner spark and I was connected to the energy of creation.

Around the Subway car, young and old from a dozen countries were seated. I realized anew we were all brothers and sisters. Somehow we had forgotten our common heritage and were connected by the Light. We allowed self-interest to blind us from this elemental truth.

When the inner song was alive in your heart, there was no room for self-interest, only love and the Light. The Light was the magical element; it was the force that held everything together and was all loving and kind. We had allowed our baser nature to lead. Deep within we knew what was right; we let fear and false belief lead us away from this unifying principal.

X - Dr. Lannis

Well it's Wednesday morning and time to tell Dr. Lannis something. Sitting in his waiting room, I am worried about what to say? If I tell him the truth, I fear both Lannis and Cohen will order further tests and put me in the hospital. In-patient psychiatric evaluation is a possibility.

Similarly, if I tell Lannis nothing, he might grow concerned and delay my return to work. I miss my job and am getting restless. What to do? As the minutes tick away and I focus on a spot on the floor, an answer finally comes to me. I will tell Lannis part of the truth. I am writing down what I remember in my journal and when I am done he can read it. Then, we can talk about it. Writing it down helps me remember and piece together what happened.

Lannis might not like this, but it is the best I can do. Also, I will tell Lea the same thing. When I am finished writing, she can read about it and we can talk.

It was a beautiful, sunny, fall morning as I came out of Lannis' office and walked along Central Park West toward the Subway at 86th Street. Things had gone better than I expected; Lannis was encouraged that I continued to write down what I remembered. He said that was a very good sign and accepted waiting to discuss the trauma until I actually remembered it. Lannis stated that often he had to prompt this recall with other patients and, because I seemed to be able to do this on my own, was optimistic about my prognosis. He looked forward to reading the journal when I was done.

We spent the rest of the session discussing my marriage, graduate study and returning to work. Lannis thought I should be able to return to work in a few weeks, but would know for certain after reading and discussing my journal.

XI - A Lesson

Although it was a holiday, Lea had to work. Having completed my schoolwork for the week, much of the day was my own and I took the subway into Manhattan. It was a sunny day and I went for a long, leisurely walk in Central Park.

Before I realized it, it was mid-afternoon and I needed to return home to complete some errands before dinner. Briskly, I began walking toward the subway.

Continuing along Central Park West, I saw a homeless man sitting on a bench. I thought to myself, this fellow looks tired and hungry. Spotting a street vendor up ahead, a thought occurred to me. Let me buy this fellow a hot pretzel to eat.

After paying for the pretzel and a small carton of orange drink, I approached the man. As I placed the pretzel, drink and napkin on the bench beside him, I said, "Here's something to eat." Angrily, the fellow looked at me and replied, "I'm not hungry. Who do you think you are?"

At this point, the fellow knocked the pretzel and the drink off the bench onto the ground. Quickly, two pigeons began tearing into their late morning snack. Feeling rebuked and not knowing what to say, I just looked at the fellow and walked away.

As I rode the Subway north to the Bronx, I wondered about the homeless fellow. Somehow, my charitable act turned into a confrontation. Why?

XII - Why Are You Here?

It was Saturday morning and I was again seated in Amoun's office. As was his way, Amoun offered me a cup of coffee, asked if I was comfortable and inquired, "So, why are you here?" Having learned from our previous exchange, I answered differently. "To find God," I replied.

Amoun looked at me and smiled, "That's a little better, but is not the reason. I have something you need and this need pulls you toward me. This need can only be filled by the Light. The Light calls to the spark within you; the spark needs to be rekindled. Like calls to like. The answer to this question cannot be spoken; it must be experienced and perceived. That is why you come here. To experience the Light and awaken that which has been asleep.

"When last we met, you experienced the Beloved's Caress and now know what you are seeking. This is only a beginning and is not the goal. It is a foretaste of future experience and preparation for something finer and more useful. There is an emptiness inside of you and the Light will fill it so that you might better work and serve. This realization and experience can only occur when the traveler is ready. A preparation is necessary. The Light of understanding will remove the cobwebs of selfish living that surround your heart. You are the obstacle that stands in your way. The Teacher's job is to show all of this to you and give you the tools necessary to travel on your own. The end result is service and love of God."

Amoun continued, "Tell me about the homeless one."
Startled, I questioned, "How did you know about that?"
"The Teacher knows everything he needs to know to help the student. All things are recorded and available to those who need to know. In time and space, there is no beginning or end; it is a continuum that starts in the past, continues in the present and reaches into the future. That which has happened is recorded and that which is about to occur is a potential. The future is not fixed. The Teacher has access to assist the student. Now, tell me about the homeless one."

"Well, I had the day off and went for a walk in Central Park. I was feeling pretty good and thought to spread my good feelings about by trying to help another. This fellow seemed hungry so I bought him something to eat."

"Then what happened," said Amoun.

"The fellow rejected my help and threw the pretzel and drink on the ground. Immediately, pigeons went after the food."

"So, what did you learn from this?"

Somewhat puzzled I replied, "What do you mean learned from it?"

"You were supposed to learn something. That was why the gift was rejected."

Stammering, I continued, "I was supposed to learn something...That was why the gift was rejected...What do you mean?...The situation was engineered?"

"The point of life is to learn and grow closer to the Light. We do this so we might better serve. In this act, your gift was rejected because it was based upon your need and not the need of the situation. You felt good so you wanted to help another. Yet, you did not question if you could be of help. You assumed, based upon previous experience, you could be helpful. This was not the case; you in fact did not know how to help. You made an assumption and did not do the necessary work. You did not inquire if the fellow was hungry.

"This rebuke was to teach you. Today, when you come here you come with assumptions. These are based upon previous learning and in this endeavor are baggage. You think that by coming here and asking questions you will get answers, but you are not yet fitted for the answers. You have not done the necessary work, which is examining your assumptions. How do you know you can benefit from this situation, because you think you can?

"It is only the Light that has the real knowledge in this matter. So, you were called here to begin the process of learning.

"For an action to be beneficial, it must be the right time, in the right place, with the right people."

XIII - A Walk in the Park

It was a clear, fall morning and Amoun wanted to go for a walk. Entering Washington Square Park, Amoun pointed to a bench, in the sunlight, overlooking the large cement circle and meeting space in the park's center. The park was alive with activity: children playing with a colorful beach ball, young parents pushing babes in strollers, vendors selling hot dogs, pretzels, and peanuts, and street people waking from their night in and around the bathroom lawn.

As we came to rest beside an empty bench, Amoun looked-up at the sun and took a long, deep breath. Slowly, he smiled and said, "God is Kind." Together we both sat quietly and observed the variety of activity about us. People were going and doing, exploring all of the fun things to do in the park.

By this time, the street people were up and about. Some had started to pan handle from willing strangers and others purchased drugs from pushers. Then, an old man caught my attention. He was struggling, walking slowly with the aid of a walker; a middle age, female attendant assisted with words of encouragement. I enjoyed the variety of late morning activity and wondered to myself, what is the point of all this going and doing? To what purpose is all this activity?

Amoun looked at me and replied, "this entire splendor sings the praise of the Light. Each going and doing; enjoying, suffering, laughing, struggling and moving forward in their own way. While some are lost in the shadows for a time, on another day, in a different place, they may embrace the Light. That is the point of the journey. That is the point of the friction between darkness and the Light. The friction, or struggle, exists to push us forward.

"Like this park, the world is a giant bazaar. You will find in it exactly what you are looking for. Some seek enjoyment of the senses. Others seek responsibility and family. Does this make one right and the other wrong? No, it is not like that. While many activities and choices are harmful and must be avoided, their real impact is that they distance the traveler from the Light. The flesh is weak and must fade, however, the spirit lives on. Remember, the real or lasting meaning of an endeavor is if it brings you closer to or distances you from the

Light. This measuring stick, or internal indicator, awakens as the traveler progresses.

"How can we evaluate the importance of a life? How do we know the outcome of years spent in the darkness? If the traveler can only awaken after years of being in the darkness, is he not like you and I? Was it not dark last night and this morning the sun caresses our skin? Does not the Light follow the darkness?"

By this time, I no longer listened to Amoun's words. I had become absorbed by the peaceful, loving energy that emanated from him and carried the words. Somehow, by being in Amoun's presence, I was transported to that peaceful, loving place that I now recognized as the goal of the journey. As Amoun reflected the Light, I perceived my own connection to the Light and recognized the Light in everything about me. This energy was the very fabric of life and we were created to know and serve the Light.

XIV - Submission

I do not remember the ride home on the subway. It remains a blur. However, I do remember getting home late that afternoon.

When I entered our apartment, Lea was busy cleaning; she had just gotten home from work at the Nursing Home and I could see that she was angry with me.

"Sorry I'm late," I said, hoping to avoid what was coming.

Lea stopped dusting and replied in an angry tone, "If you were running late, why didn't you call? I was worried."

"I do not know. I got caught up with things down at NYU and lost track of time."

Hearing my excuse, Lea got even more annoyed, "That's not a good reason. I need you to vacuum and go shopping for groceries. Our guests will be here at 7:30 p.m. and we don't even have the chicken and other ingredients to start dinner. If you had called, I could have told you to pick up a few things before coming home. Now what are we going to serve them?"

"I don't know. Maybe I can get some Chinese food or pizza?"

Then, Lea began to cry and said through her tears, "You know, I support your work. Going to school and working at the hospital is difficult, but I need you here as well. I have a job and count on you for things too. Tonight's dinner is going to be a mess!"

Lea sobbed and I didn't know what to do. I stood there for a moment and finally mumbled, "I'm sorry. I should have called. Let me run down to the grocery store and get a few things so we can start dinner. When I get back I'll vacuum."

Quickly closing the apartment door, I walked down the steps and could still hear Lea crying. Continuing on, I wondered why this was happening. Perhaps, if Lea knew about Amoun, she would understand that I am doing something more important than shopping and vacuuming?

Sitting down on the front steps of the building, my emotions began to build up. I felt ashamed that I hurt Lea and avoided my responsibilities, but didn't Lea know I was one of the chosen?

Then, amidst my tears and confusion, I heard a stern command resonate through my consciousness. This voice was unlike anything I had ever experienced. "If you cannot submit to this woman, how are you going to submit to me?"

Startled and frightened, I wondered where this voice was coming from. Was I now having auditory hallucinations? Or was it my higher consciousness making a very strong point? I hoped I was not losing my mind.

Without hesitation, I picked myself up from the steps, went back into the apartment and apologized to Lea again. Meaning it this time, I told her that she was right and I should have called, that it was wrong for me to leave her with all the work. Softly, I kissed her on the cheek and asked for forgiveness.

As I sit and write this down in my journal, I am not sure what is real and what is imagined. Did this actually happen? Or, did I make it up? In my work I have seen many with religious preoccupations believing God speaks to them.

Oh, the line between reality and imagination is a fine one.

What will I tell Lannis? What will I tell Lea? What do I tell myself about all of this? Perhaps, when it is all written down it will make more sense?

XV - The Teacher's Job

Walking out of the Subway station at St. Mark's Place, I was excited. I had been anticipating this Saturday morning meeting with Amoun all week.

When I entered the bookstore and asked the young woman behind the counter if I could see Amoun, she replied, "He's not here." For a moment I was disappointed, then she continued, "Amoun left a note for you."

Nervously, I opened the envelope and read, "meet me in the park, Amoun."

Breathing a sigh of relief and grateful Amoun had not forgotten me, I thanked the young woman.

Walking through the streets toward Washington Square Park, I was struck by all of the activity. People of every age, shape and size, going and doing. Each with their own lives filled with hopes and cares. Yet, each connected by an inner reality that was more loving and caring than they could imagine.

Somehow, we had lost our connection with this Reality; this was our birthright and balancing factor. This Reality, or Light, bound all things together and enabled us to operate in the world. Without this Reality we would wither and die. According to Amoun, "it was the life Force and mother and father of us all."

Entering Washington Square Park this morning, I saw the park a little differently. Here, in this quiet, green place, amidst one of the largest cities in the world was an opportunity to be whatever you wanted. In a small way, the park was a representation of our lives. For me, this place became a center of spiritual learning. For the young child, it was a place to play. Senior citizens came here to meet their friends, play chess and feed the pigeons. Waiting for class, college students learned about love. Street people took care of business and sought to ease the pain of their lives.

Walking further, I saw Amoun. He was seated on a bench in the far right corner of the park; the bench was next to the area where the chess players met daily to test themselves against each other. As I approached, Amoun opened his eyes and said, "Welcome, I see you got my note. It was too nice to sit inside. I will miss the sun. I hope you do not mind?"

I replied, "I like sitting in the park. There are so many people to watch and wonder about."

Getting down to business Amoun questioned, "So why are you here?"

Never knowing how to answer this question and afraid I would give the wrong answer, hesitantly, I replied, "To learn and grow closer."

Amoun questioned further, "What else?"

After three different responses concerning recent events in my life I offered, "I heard this voice in my head which said…"

Before I could finish Amoun replied, "I know about that…What did you learn from this experience? What was its point?"

Surprised by this I muttered, "I do not know." Over the last few days, I had numerous thoughts about this, ranging from how lucky I was to have a spiritual experience to thinking that I'm losing my mind. Also, I wondered who was chastising me. Again, I never considered I was supposed to learn something from it.

I questioned Amoun, "How did you know about that?"

In a very serious tone Amoun said, "It is the Teacher's job to know about the student and protect them. This was given so you would learn from it. It was not given so you could feel special or chosen. Perhaps, you wondered if you were crazy or hearing voices like those people you work with?

"It is not like this. You are to learn, then move on. Spiritual experiences are given to help us learn. Experiences and capacities are not the end of the search. They are road signs to follow. The destination is submission to the Light and service as a servant of the Light. That is the goal. That is the destination.

"Standing in the way of reaching this destination are thoughts, desires and assumptions. They are part of every day conditioning and are necessary to participate in the world. Yet they block the door. You must learn to still for a time all these distractions so you can approach the door and open it. All of these capacities are within you. It is the Teacher's job to show these things to you and guide your progress.

"Within, you have all that you need to make the journey. Capacities that both hinder and help you succeed. When first you came to me, I showed you your own inner Light and, in accord with the Divine Plan, I reflected the Light upon your heart and you were reborn. That first day, you were aglow with your own inner capacity as it sang the song of creation. You were joined with the Light of the universe.

"In part, what we do each time we meet, I help you recognize your own inner roadblocks. These obstacles stand in the way of you reaching the door. These desires and assumptions fill your consciousness and never still; they prevent you from hearing your own inner song and the song of the universe. You are always connected to the Light, but do not realize it.

"The voice you heard was your own higher nature instructing your lower nature to be still and submit to the situation. In this matter, the Light guided your higher nature. The situation was about helping your wife take care of things, but it was much more. The entire journey is encapsulated in that experience."

Amoun continued speaking about many things; my soul was absorbed in the peaceful Light that emanated from him and that is all that I remember.

After a time Amoun said, "Come, we have work to do."

Reluctantly, I roused myself from the spiritual reverie and followed. Amoun was walking toward the street people who were sitting on the grass adjacent to the park bathrooms. Walking at a brisk pace, he was reaching into his pocket and pulling out a roll of money.

Approaching the dozen or so people who made their home in this portion of the park, I wondered what Amoun was going to do. As he went from person to person, he called each by name, offered a few words of personal encouragement and gave a few dollars. With each gift, he said, "Here, use this to care for yourself as the sunshine cares for your body."

Each of the homeless ones looked at him with kindness and wonder. They had not requested anything; Amoun went over to them and gave. Even from a distance, I heard a few of the people whisper, "Thank you, Amoun." After five minutes, Amoun had given all that he had.

As we walked back toward the bookstore, I could see some of the homeless ones getting up to purchase hot-dogs and pretzels from the vendors. Others were hurrying toward the liquor store and pushers to buy a little happiness.

From the manner in which the homeless people responded I could see this was not the first time Amoun emptied his pockets. They were comfortable with his approach and grateful for the help offered. While we made our way back to the bookstore, I did not know what to say.

"How is your coffee?" asked Amoun.

"Fine," I replied.

Amoun took a sip of his coffee and we sat enjoying the silence. Then Amoun continued with the lesson.

"You see, most people make a show of giving to another. They want their name in the newspaper or a sign on the wall dedicated to them. Yet, giving to those in need is a basic requirement of being a human being. There is nothing special to giving to those in need; it is a social duty to others. Wanting recognition for doing your duty is wishing to get paid twice for the same activity. Our payment is the good feelings we get and knowing that we are trying to help another. This is a basic requirement of life; we must try to help our brother. If someone is hungry, shouldn't we try to feed them?"

I replied, "Yes. I understand but some of those people were using your money to buy liquor and drugs, but isn't that wrong; providing the opportunity for someone to hurt themselves?"

Amoun looked deeply into my eyes and continued in a serious tone, "Does not the sun shine for everyone? If some choose to lie in the sun for hours without proper sunscreen and develop illness, is the sun to fault? Should the sun refuse to shine because some choose to misuse it? What about all the others who draw life and sustenance from the life giving rays?"

With an embarrassed look on my face, I realized how limited my view of the situation had been.

Amoun continued, "In this matter there are two aspects to consider. First, giving to others is a natural part of life and is a basic requirement of the universe. Without giving there would be no life or existence as we know it. What you saw today was at the lower range of the continuum; there are many forms of giving which are at a higher and finer level.

"One example is giving without the person asking. The giver perceives the need and gives anonymously. In this way, the recipient is not indebted to a particular person and is prevented the embarrassment of having to ask. This is only one example and on the spiritual level, there are higher levels to giving. The point of my explanation is that you made more of this activity than is necessary. My giving to those people was not a spiritual activity but a social duty. It was part of my basic responsibility as a human being.

"Because some wish to confuse social duty with spiritual activity, I do not have to be limited by this model.

"Second, the fact that some choose to use what they have been given to harm themselves, in this matter that is beyond my control. I give because they are in need and the fact that some choose to kill pain of their lonely life with alcohol and drugs is between them and their God. Perhaps, one day, these poor souls will reach higher and I will be there for them as I am here for you. Who can tell the destiny of a life? Each comes to God in their time.

"I did not create these people or the circumstances that led them to make their home in the park. I cannot judge their pain or suffering and do not know the outcome of their life. Spiritually, they are in the hands of another who loves them more than you or I can love them. God is always there and will be waiting when they are ready to come home. Today, my duty to them was a social duty nothing more. In this matter, there are limitations to my activity."

XVI - Journal Entry

Riding home on the #6 Train to the Bronx, I have time to consider all that has happened to me.

Over the last few weeks, I have begun graduate school and been accepted in one of the finest universities in the land. This is something I have worked toward for years.

Additionally, for some unknown reason, I have been accepted into an advanced study of another kind. This training specializes in higher capacities of the mind and focuses on how to use the Light to help others. Somehow, this training sought me out and my teacher, Amoun, has capacities and spiritual abilities that appear supra-normal to me. In my Saturday meetings with him, the way I look at the world has been completely changed.

Writing this entry in my journal, I remain unclear about this part. I know I have forgotten something and once I remember it, I will be able to continue with my life. Dr. Lannis maintains I have suffered a severe shock and must remember the event before the healing is complete.

To resume all normal duties and the stress of work, before I remember the event, puts the healing process at risk. Should something happen at work to trigger the recall I could relapse and become disoriented again, perhaps for good. Dr. Lannis is concerned the shock may in some way be connected to work; I know it is not. Somehow it is connected to my relationship with Amoun. That's why it is good that I keep writing what I can remember.

During all of this, Lea remains supportive and loving. She encourages me to write, knowing I will unlock the key to the mystery in this way. Lea does not press me about what I am writing and is content to wait for me to share it. Fortunately, I have been granted sick leave from the hospital and do not have to worry about the bills. This leave pays my salary and, as long as I keep my appointments with Lannis and keep him happy, I do not have to worry about money.

Also, going to graduate school one evening a week gives me something meaningful to do. This study will be useful in my career and I enjoy the mental stimulation of it.

To get better, I write in this journal and try to recall what triggered my disorientation. Something happened in those Saturday morning sessions that caused me to go crazy…What was it?

XVII - The Path

Amoun inquired, "How is your coffee?"

"Fine, it is just the way I like it."

"Good, now let us get down to business. Why have you come?"

"To learn and grow closer to the Light."

At this, Amoun smiled and began the lesson. "Each person comes to the Light in their own time. Once they have found the object of their search, the flame of love is kindled in their heart. Mercifully, they have found the object of the search and are no longer empty and alone. As the love matures and they experience more of the Light, all the traveler wishes is to serve and be one with the Light.

"This is the ancient path of love of God; it is the basis for all religious systems and all religions are joined at this level of spiritual experience. It is on a worldly level that religions differ and people argue. Internally, religions are united in this oneness of spirit. This way of submission to the Light is always available in all countries and towns. Remember this path is not for everyone.

"You and I have spent time in the park. We have encountered many people of varying ages and backgrounds. Each is a traveler and has come into this realm to learn, work and serve. Depending upon their destiny and how much work they have done as preparation, they advance toward this inner realization. Each is a soul that has been given a mission to go out into the universe to learn, work and serve. The return journey back to the Light begins the moment the soul embraces the Light. This is the object of the search; this is the treasure of all the legends and is the pot of gold at rainbow's end.

"Without Divine intervention, this realization cannot be given to anyone. Additionally, it has to be earned through a preparation of search and sincere longing. What the traveler brings is sincerity and an open mind. Healthy skepticism and pure heart are essential requirements. Because the heart is pure and the traveler seeks the answer for its own sake, skepticism, intellectual curiosity and self-interest can be suspended for a time. During this brief suspension of the intellect, under the direction of the Teacher, the flame of love is rekindled in the heart and the traveler experiences the awakening of the soul.

"That is what the Teacher brings to the situation; the capacity to awaken what has been asleep. This is only done when the traveler has been prepared with purity of heart and balancing of intellectual capacity. This balancing includes skepticism and the capacity to suspend this skepticism so spiritual learning can occur. In part, preconceived notions about spiritual experience block learning.

"The question was in your mind, why does not Amoun offer this wondrous Teaching to those unfortunate ones in the park? Surely, this magical Light cannot hurt them; it can only help their condition. Why does Amoun only offer these unfortunates a few dollars?

"First, they are not ready and would not accept the Teaching. Second, you make unfair judgments about these people. How do you know the spiritual condition of these people? Is it not possible they are of a higher spiritual degree than you and I? Perhaps, some assume this garb so they will not be bothered by the chains of this world. Do you think the one who refused your pretzel was merely a bum? You are quick to judge by externals.

"The Light loves these people and loves you as well. Each comes to God and the ultimate reason for existence, when they are ready. To come any sooner causes lasting harm.

"I give to them as I give to you. Just as I project the Light upon your heart so I project it to them as well. To most, this experience is hidden, perceived on a level that you term unconscious. Because you have awakened, you can perceive the Light on a more conscious level, but only in measured amounts. On a cloudy day, the sun is always shining and is available to all. Yes, I give them the opportunity to awaken; yet, they are not ready. Their worldly needs and desires block the inner Light from shinning forth. Because of your effort and the grace of the Path, you were ready to awaken. That is why you perceived the inner call. You had done the work and were able to accept the Light on its own terms. You do not seek power and position from this learning; you wish to learn and serve because you love.

"In this way, the secret protects itself. The treasure cannot be found without seeking and will never be found unless the seeker is pure of heart and free of self-interest. Love is not concerned with magical powers and fine position; it is about nearness and desire to serve.

"Just as the sunlight is available to all, so the Light of creation shines down on everyone. Daily, the Servants of God reflect the Light into all parts of the world. This Light is life sustaining and protects us all from our own inner darkness. The Light protects, enables and sustains; without it we would wither and die. Similarly, the Light enables the Plan for humanity; as each soul reaches upward, so humanity is evolving to a higher condition.

"This evolution is of mind and consciousness. Each can become something higher and finer, assisting others to embrace their own inner potential. In order for this to happen, the darkness or self-interest in each soul must be balanced. That is, in part, the job of the Light; the Light is the enabling factor and a nutrient for our souls.

"Always, the higher soul is in contact with the Light. Most people are unaware of this contact, as it is on a deep, inner level. Yet, when one is ready to awaken, this realization becomes part of the ordinary consciousness. Under the guidance of a Teacher, the spiritual consciousness comes forward. In time, as the traveler progresses, both the everyday and spiritual consciousness are present in the mind together.

"And as an individual soul can awaken and embrace the Light, that is the ultimate destiny of humanity. One day, everyone will accept this reality. That is the point of the Teaching."

And as I sat and listened to these words, they rang true. My soul celebrated and spiritually embraced their message. Yes, God was love and each soul is provided the opportunity to embrace a cosmic potential. We are all brothers and sisters and for selfish reasons have forgotten this.

Wars, injustice, and greed were the makings of our own inner darkness. We were given the opportunity to both create and destroy. If we reached higher, we could become masters of our own inner kingdom and the world would be a better place.

Fortunately, there was something higher and finer than us to help guide; the Light which watches over us and keeps us from totally giving in to our baser nature. We could choose to make the world a better place. First, we had to work on ourselves and learn to turn toward the Light. After we master ourselves we could truly help make the world a better place. The key to a better world is better people and better people are made one person at a time.

Higher capacities of the mind and perception of the Light are part of each person's destiny. This is the hidden treasure. This is the destiny of humanity.

Why had we forgotten? Why had we lost sight of the fact that we were all one family connected through the Light?

As if hearing my inner questions, Amoun continued. "The struggle between darkness and Light exists within each soul. The darkness is the call of our baser nature and is most easily characterized by self-interest. While the right degree of self-interest is good and necessary, some make self-interest the overriding factor. This greed or desire to have whatever one wants whenever they want it, can become destructive to ourselves and others.

"Often greed blocks the door to higher study and keeps the traveler at a lower level. In higher studies, the capacity to suspend for a time, self-interest and intellectual satisfaction is necessary. The higher impulse will not operate when this part of the mind is functioning.

"In our view, darkness is that which takes you away from your own higher nature; Light is that which leads you to your own capacity to be one with the Light. That which is good is that which leads you to your own inner song and submission to the Light. That which is bad is that which distances you from your own inner Light.

"The struggle or friction between darkness and Light is necessary to the journey. It is this friction and contrast that pushes the traveler on. Without this friction, often we would not reach our full potential.

"Similarly, the contrast between the worldly and spiritual is fundamental to the process. The magical element is the Light and grace of the path. Without this mercy, none would be saved from their own lower-self. When the Light is reflected upon the heart, the soul knows which way to turn. This mercy is extended to us and is the ladder we need to climb higher. Without this enabling factor each would be lost in a haze of self-deception.

"The grace of the path and how to embrace our own higher nature, is a mercy for everyone."

XVIII - A Suggestion

As I continue writing these things down and describing Amoun's teaching, I am unsure where it will lead. So far, all that I remember is both joy and wonder. What happened that unsettled me so? Didn't Amoun say, "The student was protected from spiritual harm by the grace of the path?"

At this point, I cannot remember anything that comes close to being harmful. Yet, I was in a daze for six days and cannot remember what happened. Where am I going with all of this?

Amoun's teaching is a wonderful philosophy of life.

While Lea and I were walking toward our friend's apartment on 96th Street, Lea inquired how my treatment with Dr. Lannis was progressing. I told her that I had been writing more frequently in my journal.

"Have you remembered anything yet?"

Trying to be evasive I replied, "A little."

"Is there anything you can share with me?"

"No, not really. I am waiting to remember it all before talking with Lannis about it."

"Oh, you don't want to speak with me first? You know that hurts. I have been worried ever since this thing happened, thinking all kinds of thoughts. As your wife, I should know what happened first."

Seeing that Lea was hurt, I stopped walking and gave her a hug. "If it will make you feel better I can tell you some things. I have not worked it all out. It's not about another woman, sex or drugs. It seems to be connected to a person I met down at NYU. He runs a bookstore and I would stop by and talk with him about spiritual matters. As far as I can tell, something happened with him that was unsettling and I became lost for days."

"Since this thing happened, have you spoken to this man? Perhaps he can help you remember what happened?"

Lea's question stopped me from walking any further. I paused for a moment and replied, "What a great idea. No, I have not even thought about doing that. Each week when I go to class…"

I stopped talking and forced myself to remember. When I got off the train at St. Mark's Place, I did not walk past the bookstore. I walked down 9th Street, past Broadway and made my left turn toward the Main Building by Washington Square Park. I had been avoiding the bookstore. Why?

Standing in front of our friend's building, Lea could see that she said something important and looked worried.

I reached for her hand. Walking inside I replied, "Thanks. You triggered a memory. That really helped me."

Feeling better Lea replied, "You know I love you and am worried. I want to be part of your life and will do anything to help. Please include me. I have enjoyed your being home and helping with the household chores. In some strange way, I think this thing has brought us closer together."

Walking inside the elevator, I gave Lea a kiss on the cheek and said, "I love you too."

XIX - Dr. Lannis' Office

Back in Dr. Lannis' office, it was time for me to get my head shrunk again.

"How's the journal going?" began Lannis.

"I'm still writing and things are getting clearer by the day. In fact, Lea and I were discussing what happened and she helped me remember something I had kept hidden."

"Want to talk about it?"

"No, not really…but I was wondering what you thought about or knew about higher perceptions of the mind?"

"I'm not sure what you are asking me?"

Typical shrink response; avoid answering the question directly and get the patient to elaborate. I was the one who started this, so I went on a little further. "I'm talking about higher capacities or abilities of the mind. Things like knowing the future, reading someone's mind, or precognition that something will happen. What do you know about this sort of thing?"

"Why, has something like this happened to you?"

Still avoiding answering the question; always turning it back to me. I continued, "No, nothing has happened that I can remember. But recently I met someone who seemed to have some of these abilities and we became friends. For a time, we would meet and discuss these things. For the most part, that's what I have been writing about in my journal. What are your thoughts about spiritual or higher capacities of the mind? Have you ever studied in this area?"

For a moment, Lannis sucked on his pipe while he thought about how to respond. In an earlier session, Lannis informed me he gave up smoking and used the pipe as a prop and for support. As Lannis played with his pipe, I could see that he was trying to work out what to say.

Tired of waiting I blurted out, "Well! Have you anything to say about this or not?"

Lannis smiled, took the pipe out of his mouth and began. "You know, it's not really important what I think about all of this but what you think. That's the bottom line. If this is the thing which pushed you over and caused you to be lost to yourself for most of a week, then it's important.

Lannis continued, "In the emergency room, all of your blood tests came back negative for drugs and we quickly ruled out abduction or forced sexual contact. You were clean and had no bruises of any kind. In fact, you were as healthy as could be. You had no signs of exposure like most street people. It was like you were protected from harm or kept in a safe place for a week. Certainly, we were puzzled and considered someone gave you shelter. So, it's about a spiritual cult? Were you held by some kind of cult and escaped?"

I started to laugh and Lannis seemed surprised. "Why are you laughing?"

"Well, when people talk about spiritual awareness and higher capacities of the mind, stereotypically that's their first reaction. Because most people have had such few genuine spiritual experiences, all they can relate to outside of traditional Christian and Judaic teaching is cult phenomena. I'm talking about the real thing. Do you think it is possible to have genuine spiritual experience and develop higher capacities of the mind?"

With a challenge in his voice, Lannis replied, "Our wards in the psychiatric hospital are filled with people who claim this sort of thing. In your work as well as mine, you see what this has done to people."

"Typical scientific bullshit," I replied. "You still haven't answered the question."

Finally, Lannis said, "yes, I think it is possible and probable. Most cultures acknowledge this phenomena and western psychiatry is beginning to examine this area as well. Today scientists and psychiatrists are convinced these experiences are worthy of study and, in this area, we don't have many answers. Eastern traditions are more familiar with this phenomenon and have been working in this area for years. Eastern students assert mastery in areas western scientists, until recently, did not even know existed.

"Western research and inquiry into these phenomena have a number of structural limitations and flaws. First, because higher capacities of the mind do not lend themselves easily to scientific inquiry as we know it in the west, it has been difficult for western scientists and psychiatrists to investigate this area. These capacities seem to come and go under a set of circumstances we do not yet understand; they cannot be easily controlled and replicated in the laboratory. They seem to exist as an organic part of life. Second, this area is filled with pretenders and charlatans. It is difficult to know the true from the false."

As I sat there thinking about what Lannis said, I thought to myself, somehow I had come across the real thing, the genuine article. The more I thought about it, the clearer it became; I was never going to be the same.

XX - Lessons

As we sat in the park and watched the different people, Amoun pointed out the fellow I noticed weeks before with a walker. He was an older, frail gentleman, attended by the same middle-age woman. Sitting on a bench in the sun, the older man appeared to enjoy the fresh air.

Slowly Amoun spoke, "Sickness is the great teacher, for it reminds us the flesh must perish and to search for something lasting. Through illness, some grow meaner and others more gentle and loving. Who can say which of us will become sour or sweet through adversity? Or, who will use the opportunity to join with our lasting, transcendent nature? Remember that this life, in part, is a preparation for the next; we continue the learning and service throughout the realms.

"You come to me because I have something you need. I, too, benefit from our relationship and use the opportunity to grow closer to my lasting self. In our learning, there is no time and space. We are joined in spirit and not bound by the physical laws. Ultimately, we are creatures of spirit and learn to rise upward toward our lasting selves joined as brothers in the Light and cannot be separated in this respect.

"One day, each must close their eyes to this world and travel on. The spiritual learning in this world is a preparation for the next. Here, because of the pull of the physical world, we can accelerate the return journey. Because of the contrast between the physical and spiritual, we learn quicker.

"Inside is a whisper, an impulse, that is our higher nature trying to communicate. This impulse is hidden below all the other noises that fill our consciousness: the physical cravings of the body, the ideas in our head, and emotions requiring expression. Each noise in its own way covering the inner whisper. Once the consciousness has been stilled and the inner whisper has grown strong, spiritually the traveler is better able to serve.

"In order to balance the consciousness and still, for a time, the noises in our head, the traveler must learn to identify and disarm his thoughts and feelings. For it is these ideas, conditioning and strong emotions that block the higher consciousness. Through the guidance of the Teacher, slowly the traveler learns to unravel the layers of consciousness that block the door and push them aside. In those moments, the higher consciousness operates. The traveler has stilled that which requires stilling and the higher impulse is set free and comes forward. In this state, it is said the traveler has arrived and reached full consciousness. In most, this is not a static condition.

"Always, on an inner level, we are connected to the Light. This is part of who we are and with proper guidance can bring this realization to full consciousness.

"In this matter, it is not a question of adding something but removing that which blocks the way. Our desires and preconceptions block the higher impulse from fully awakening and operating.

"When one has arrived or reached the goal of spiritual seeking, it is said the traveler has died to himself or herself and awakened to their higher consciousness. The death, which is being described, is the death of self or desire so that which is hidden might come forward. These perfected ones are transparent in that their individual needs no longer exist; they are one with the Light and their higher self. In most, this is a transitory condition and exists for brief periods. For those more advanced, this condition is more permanent.

"Most people go through life and fear death, or the cessation of the physical body. On the path, there is a death which precedes this; it is the death of self that is tied to the world. As a result of this, the spirit awakens while in the body. This is the goal of the mystical process and the point of the Teaching.

"Through the intervention of the Teacher and the Mercy of the Path, the fire of love kindles in the heart. Slowly, the inner Light is awakened and the fire burns from within pushing its way outward. As the fire burns outward, it melts our connection to the world and our desire for things. These needs and desires take a secondary position to the spiritual burning. When we are fully awake we have both sets of consciousness in our minds. We perceive the physical and spiritual, intuitively knowing what each situation requires."

"Come, let us go for a walk," said Amoun. And we began walking toward the bathroom lawn where the homeless lived and slept through the night. As we grew closer, the homeless men and women began to stir and call out, "Amoun, Amoun. Here I am."

One by one, Amoun gave money to each of them and in a matter of moments each was gone. Some going back to their spot on the lawn and others going off to buy what they needed.

Then Amoun turned to me and said, "How about some hot chocolate and a warm pretzel. One block over, there is a vendor who makes the best hot chocolate and his pretzels are soft and fresh."

"Sure, I would like some." We walked south just past the student union. Amoun was right. The hot chocolate was sweet and the pretzels were warm and soft. Enjoying both, we walked back to the bookstore and into the rear office.

After we finished our food, Amoun continued with the lesson. "Life is a wonderful opportunity and is to be enjoyed. There are many things to fill our senses, give us pleasure and make us happy. God provides a family, friends, clothing and food. It is up to us to make something of this opportunity and enjoy our life.

"Many make of religion too serious a thing. They are confused and believe we can only grow closer through seriousness, hard work, and giving things up. Yes, we can make progress in this way but where is the joy and laughter? Who says the road is only paved with seriousness and piety?

"Religion is a song that arises from your heart and is a joy that fills your days. There should be no compulsion in religion. Prayers should be offered out of love, laughter and joy.

"Is not offering a cup of hot chocolate an act of giving; is this not a holy thing? Who is the creator of this hot chocolate? Giving in His Name is it not an act of service, love and joy? Is not the chocolate His who created the vendor?

"When you drink deep and experience the richness of flavor is this not a prayer of thanksgiving? Many confine prayer to words and times. Any act done out of love of God is a prayer. In fact, the greatest life is the life that is lived for God.

"Now, let us speak of another matter. In our studies, time and space do not confine us. Our classroom is the world and we can communicate with our students anytime and anywhere. In the physical world, you can call someone on the West Coast using a cell phone. In the world of spirit, the Teacher can communicate with the student through the Light and, as the student becomes more fully aware of his spiritual capacities, is more able to perceive the messages.

"Over time and through the Mercy of the Path, the inner and outer consciousness become one and the student is fully aware of these impulses. Prior to this conscious awareness, the spiritual Teaching is on an inner, hidden level. In fact, most of the Teaching occurs at night when the student is asleep and not consciously aware of the learning. The worldly consciousness is not present to interfere. I do not wish to say anymore about this, other than I can communicate with you whenever I need to."

XXI - Searching for Amoun

I decided to take Lea's advice and see if Amoun could help me remember what happened. Tonight before class, I went to the bookstore to speak with him.

As I rode the Subway and thought about what I would learn, I continued to wonder, why had I been content to write about Amoun rather than visit or call him? Also, I wondered why I had not thought of this myself. Usually, I was good at solving problems. Perhaps, I was protecting myself from something?

As most of the Subway riders around me slept, these questions filled my mind.

As I left the Subway station at St. Mark's Place and walked toward Broadway, I began to grow anxious. I wondered what I would find. Would the bookstore be there? Had I made-up this story about Amoun to explain the lost days? Were the walks and talks in Washington Square Park a figment of my imagination? Did I invent an encounter with a Holy man to conceal a sinister event?

Growing closer to the bookstore, I was beginning to sweat and felt my stomach tense. With each step, I was nearer to having an anxiety attack. I needed to calm myself and began to take slow, measured breaths. Concentrating on my breathing usually helped to relax me.

Then, just up ahead I saw it: **Lightbearer Books.** My heart began to race and I quickened my pace. As I opened the door and walked into the store, I saw her and breathed a sigh of relief. I had not imagined the young woman who worked the counter. She was sorting books as I came through the door and as soon as she saw me, she smiled and said, "I wondered when you would return. I was worried about you."

I looked at her and replied, "I am confused. Perhaps, you can help me. Is Amoun here?"

Without hesitating she said, "Come with me into the office."

Quickly, I followed her through the store to the rear office. Without knocking she entered. No one was inside. I recognized the small desk, visitor's chair I often sat in and the coffeepot on the table against the wall.

Not seeing Amoun I was afraid to say anything. The young woman spoke. "You don't remember do you?"

"Only bits and pieces. Where is Amoun? Please, I have seen you here many times; who are you and where is Amoun?"

"My name is Laria. I am Amoun's youngest daughter. I don't know how to tell you this. I thought you knew. You were there. Amoun is gone. He passed over."

Shocked, I tried to absorb everything she said.

Laria continued, "Please have a seat. We can talk later, in about half-an-hour, when my relief comes in. For now, I need to go up front and take care of the store. If you want, help yourself to some coffee."

With these instructions, Laria walked out of the office toward the front of the store.

Why hadn't I noticed the resemblance between father and daughter before? Certainly, I walked past Laria enough times. Why hadn't Amoun said anything to me about his daughter? In fact, as I considered the things Amoun had said, I realized he never spoke about his personal life. All Amoun spoke about was the Teaching, the Light and my needs. Always, Amoun was focused on me.

Alone, sitting in the familiar chair in front of the desk, I began to grow sadder. I looked at the empty chair and the pot of coffee behind the desk and realized Amoun was gone. Laria said, "he passed over." Amoun was dead and tears began to fill my eyes.

And as I sat and cried, I realized I had not made-up any of this. Amoun was real and something happened that was connected to my relationship with Amoun. All along, I had been on the right track.

It was on an overcast day that we were walking through Washington Square Park and Amoun continued with the Teaching.

"Remember, in this thing there is no time and space. Each is a spark of Light that journeys from realm to realm doing the work of the Light. And after our many travels, experiences and service we return home to the Light more complete. Then, we join the Light and help shine upon the universe.

"Like you, I too am a traveler and soon must journey on. I have work in other realms and soon must leave.

"Do not be sad when these events unfold. As a servant of the Light, no spiritual harm will ever befall you; those who have gone ahead and the mercy of the Path protect us. In this work, we are brothers and sisters and are protected from lasting harm."

As I sat lost in these images, Laria returned to the office and sat down behind Amoun's desk. With a sad expression Laria continued, "You don't remember? That's why you have not been back? The others have returned. We have resumed the meetings but we did not hear from you. Now I know why."

"Please Laria, I only understand fragments. What are you talking about? The others? The meetings? Amoun never spoke about meetings or other people. Always your father and I were alone. As we sat and spoke, he imparted to me some of his wisdom.

"Now, I realize the lost days I have been trying to remember, are somehow connected to Amoun and this bookstore. Please, tell me what happened. I have not been well and need to regain my memory so I can return to work."

Laria, with her dark, black eyes looked sadly into my eyes and said, "Amoun passed over. He died nearly a month ago. Like the others, you were there when it happened. It was a miracle and, if I am not mistaken, you will help to record it and spread the Teaching.

"Now I cannot tell you more. There must be a reason you have forgotten. With Amoun's assistance, and in the way intended, you will remember. Then we can talk. Perhaps you will write it down? In this work, I am only a participant. This work emanates from a place far away and carries into the future. As is required, we participate in the plan and do our duty.

"Please, if I could tell you more I would. I am fearful that if I speak further, I will not allow for a natural healing. You must work this thing out in your own way. I am not permitted to speak further.

"It is late, do you not have someplace you need to be?"

Disappointed, I thanked Laria for her help and left to attend class.

XXII - Getting Closer

That evening when I got home, Lea was waiting anxiously to hear what happened. She knew I was going to the bookstore to speak with Amoun and hoped I would learn something from the meeting.

As I told Lea about my encounter with Laria, she listened intently and did not say a word until I was done. After I finished Laria's account and described how disappointed I was to learn of Amoun's death, Lea responded in a positive tone.

"I can understand your being sad at the loss of your friend, but why are you disappointed? Today, you learned a great deal. First, you did not make-up the whole thing. You were worried about that. Second, there are others who, in part, shared your experience. In time, they will help you deal with it. However, you must do the work of remembering yourself so you can share the event with others. This seems like a wonderful thing. What, you are disappointed because Laria did not spoon feed the answers to you? Laria told you, it would do you more harm than good.

"It seems to me you were given a great deal today."

I sat and considered what Lea said. Once again, Lea was right. I only thought about what I wanted from the situation and when events did not coincide with what I wanted, I was disappointed. I had failed to see what was actually there and what was being offered. This was considerable. I only wanted the easy way out. I did not want to work hard.

It was the following day and I was growing restless sitting in our apartment. I found the business of the day before both troubling and encouraging. Speaking with Laria confirmed I had not imagined my relationship with Amoun and, because of this relationship, probably suffered trauma and memory loss. With this information, I still could not recall part of my life.

Even more disturbing was the fact that Amoun was real and now he was gone. This meant, I could never speak with him or learn more about his spiritual path. Laria knew more than she told me and insisted I remember the details myself. All of this was very frustrating. Lea, Dr. Lannis and now Laria all said the same thing. They would be supportive and try to help but the responsibility of remembering was mine alone. This was the natural, healthy way.

It was midday. The late morning rain shower passed. I could not stand to be in the apartment any longer with my thoughts and decided to go for a walk on the tree lined bicycle path adjacent to Pelham Parkway. The path was two blocks from our apartment. Often, I walked there to think and be alone.

Most people were working so I easily found an empty bench where I could meditate. Watching the cars, trucks and buses pass helped focus my mind.

Slowly, I took a series of deep breaths to still my body and reach an open receptive place, mentally. As a thought entered my mind, I pushed it aside and refocused on the passing cars. In a matter of moments, I grew more relaxed. However, as time passed, nothing seemed to be happening. My subconscious was not coming forward. I could not force myself to remember. As Lannis said, it would happen naturally when I was ready.

Now, the sun was beginning to force its way through the clouds. Feeling encouraged by this sight, I began walking west. After walking for about 10 minutes, I saw it. There up ahead in the early afternoon sky, was a brilliant rainbow shooting across the Bronx. Arching for miles, high above the White Plains Train Station was a combination of red, green, yellow, orange, blue and white colors. In the distance, the bridge of colors descended somewhere in the middle of thousands of apartment buildings.

I was filled with hope by this sight and, as the rainbow lit-up the afternoon sky, I thought, "Somewhere at rainbow's end was the magical pot of gold the leprechaun guarded." Hadn't Amoun said, "The pot of gold was the higher capacity of the mind and the leprechaun was our baser quality?" Amoun. I was beginning to remember; the rainbow… Feeling weak and needing support, I rested on a bench.

XXIII - The Rainbow Body

Suddenly, I found myself in a bedroom, in a small apartment, near the bookstore. The bedroom was filled with people ranging in age from their late 20's to early 50's. The faces of the people were indistinct; the only person I recognized was Laria. Yet, I felt a warmth and love from everyone in the room and a deep sadness.

I was standing in the bedroom, holding a note in my hand and watching a person laying face-up in bed. It was Amoun; his eyes were closed and he was struggling to breathe. Laria was crying. I read the note in my hand; it was handwritten on bookstore stationary and said, *come to our apartment, Amoun is dying.* The address was scribbled down and it was signed, *Laria.*

I remembered being handed the note by a young man who worked the bookstore counter. Laria let me in and showed me to the bedroom…She said, through her tears, "Amoun wanted you here, at his death, to be a witness." I said nothing and continued to watch my friend who was near death as he rested on the bed.

And as I focused on the bed, something seemed to be happening in the room and with the light around Amoun's body. Slowly, the light around his body began to intensify and grow brighter. Then, the light in the room began to pulsate with a loving, joyful energy and began to change. The white light grew stronger and stronger and my vision began to blur; I could only see outlines of shapes and forms. And as the light grew stronger, I experienced inner celebration and joy.

Then, the white, pulsating light began to change. Suddenly, the room was filled with yellow, blue, orange, green, red and white beams of light that circled and danced around everyone present. As the multi-colored light filtered through me I felt even more electrical and alive.

Then, the rainbow light began to collect itself over and around Amoun's motionless body. Gradually, Amoun's still body became absorbed into the multi-colored light. Simultaneously, the light continued to pulsate, dance and engulf everyone in the room. Somehow, each of us merged with the rainbow light and our spirits floated on air. The spark of white light within each of us became part of the larger spectrum of colors. We rode and danced on this rainbow of colors for how long I cannot say; it seemed like eternity.

Suddenly, there was an enormous explosion and the light became so strong I could not see. The brightness numbed my eyes and I massaged them trying to regain my sight. After a time, my vision returned and I began to make out the images of the others in the room beside me. Gradually, I could discern their faces and determine they also were struggling to see.

Finally, I saw clearly and looked at the bed where Amoun was resting in death and he was gone. There was no trace of him. The bed was empty; there was no clothing left behind. All I could make out was a man's faint silhouette of white, clear Light that gradually dissipated into nothingness.

Somehow, through this celebration of colors, Amoun dissolved into the Light of creation. Miraculously, he had become all the colors of the rainbow and returned home on the pure Light.

How was this possible? How could the physical body dematerialize into multi-color light?

Recalling this event, I sat on the park bench unable to move. Slowly, I looked up into the sky, saw the rainbow and felt an inner calm. Yes, I too was part of the Light and the pot of gold was inside me as well. Finally, I was beginning to remember.

Later that afternoon, after I regained some of my composure, I went to the library to see what I could learn about this event. My mind needed more information to incorporate what my soul already knew and accepted. Something extraordinary and deeply spiritual had occurred and I had been a witness.

After considerable searching on the Internet, I determined that this phenomenon was called The Rainbow Body and was the transformation of the whole person into light. In rare individuals, at the point of death, the physical ascends with the spirit into the next realm. The body dissolves into the colors of the spectrum and this unity is considered evidence of advanced spiritual development. The body is transformed into light so that others witnessing or hearing of this might draw closer and understand the true, lasting nature of our being. We are of Light.

Different religious traditions have accounts of this occurring and its real significance is not material, but spiritual.

I needed time to think about all of this and why I was selected to participate. Even with this information, parts of my life remained unclear. The Police said they found me wandering the streets calling, "Amoun, Amoun." Had this experience caused me to go mad?

XXIV - I Remember

That evening, I could not sleep. I got up and went into the living room to continue writing in my journal.

I remembered being in the apartment with Laria and the others. We had just witnessed the rainbow body. Everyone was sad about Amoun's passing, yet something else was happening. Spiritually, each of us was joyous and connected. I perceived an energy in the apartment that was part of each of us; this energy was celebratory, loving and kind. It was the same energy I felt in Amoun's presence.

As the room continued to emanate with this energy, each of us sat down on the rug, closed our eyes and began to reflect this energy across our heart, to those we loved and wanted to help. No one spoke as we sat in this position for hours, reflecting the Light. This energy emanated from a Source beyond us, filled us to overflowing, then like mirrors, we reflected it out across the world to different people.

And as the Light continued to flow, we were connected to each other and people we helped in many places. Also, we were linked with all things in that we recognized in each thing the Light that was our mutual Source. This was the life force. It was always present. We had forgotten how to connect with it.

This was the tragedy of our lives. This was the missing element. We had forgotten how and why we needed to connect with our higher nature and the Light.

In this connection, all things are possible. We remember who we are and the point of the life. Everything is Light; we are all one. The different colors of the spectrum exist because they are necessary and afford each an opportunity to experience themselves in a different way. The Light is both singular and multi-level, uniting all things in the universe.

Even in the darkness, the Light exists. On the surface, it appears as if the Light is not present, yet the Light is the fabric of existence. This contrast exists so we might know the Light and recognize our Source easily. Both the darkness and the Light are one and are part of the same Source.

The world of forms, or the earth phase, exists so that we might accelerate the return journey back to our home. We are small particles of Light that have been sent out into the universe to learn, work and serve. Here, in this phase, because of the contrast between the physical and spiritual, greater opportunity exists to learn. In this realm through service our learning is accelerated. The friction between the physical and spiritual enhances the opportunity for the soul to advance.

When we journey into the next phase, we will have begun its work in this one. The next realm is spiritual and those who prepare for the journey, by developing their spiritual awareness, are better prepared.

I realize it may be a long time before I fully recall all the details of those six days. However, I am no longer worried about what I might remember. I am a child of the universe and the Light protects me.

In the morning, I will tell Lea and Dr. Lannis that I am ready to return to work. I will share my journal. Perhaps, they too will benefit from the rainbow body and Amoun's Teaching.

When the Police found me, I was remembering that beautiful moment when the Light called home its servant.

Book 2

Teddy's Last Swim in Paradise Land

****

And the student sat before the Master and questioned, "Happiness is a transitory thing. It is as illusive as a spring day in winter. One moment I am laughing and the next sad. Master, tell me what I must do to balance myself and find lasting happiness?"

And the Master sat, with eyes closed, for what seemed like an hour to the young student. Finally, the Master opened his eyes and softly spoke, "True and lasting happiness is found by immersing yourself in the river of your soul and, when the water has changed you, helping others." One of the great ones has said, 'A happy man thinks happy thoughts.' Yet, how do you get to a place where you think only happy thoughts? That is the mystery. It was not until I immersed myself in my own river and was changed, did I fully understand how this was possible."

In the ensuing silence, the student wondered how long he had to swim in the water of his soul before he experienced an answer.

****

I – Introduction

I first met Teddy (Theodore) Polinski 25 years ago. At the time, I was working as a Therapist in one of New York State's psychiatric hospitals. Weekly, Teddy and his wife, Helen, came to visit their son Scott. At an early age, Scott was afflicted with schizophrenia and as he grew into manhood, was one of the people the psychiatrists just did not know how to help. They tried different combinations of medication but found little to restore Scott. In the minds of the doctors, Scott was hopelessly crazy and would spend the rest of his days hearing voices and stopping in front of office doors to perform hand and foot rituals.

At first, Teddy and I were not close; it was a professional relationship. We saw each other in the treatment team meetings where Helen and he would learn about Scott's progress. Our friendship developed years later.

When we first met, my job was to report on Scott's participation in recreation activities and answer questions the Polinski's had about their son's behavior. At the end of team meetings, I would escort Helen and Teddy to the visitor's room. Here they shared a homemade meal with Scott. Always, the Polinski's brought Scott's favorite food and he was excited for days in anticipation.

Of the two parents, Helen was more forceful and asked most of the questions. From his behavior in team meetings, it was clear that Teddy reluctantly came along; he was impatient and wanted to get the visits over with as quickly as possible. I was sympathetic to Teddy's situation. The madness and behavior on the wards of a psychiatric hospital make even the strongest person uncomfortable.

In team meetings, I learned how the Polinski family interacted and dealt with Scott's illness. They both fought to get their son the best treatment available. Scott was the eldest of two children and developed childhood schizophrenia. He never got past first grade and was going to special classes by the age of eight. Sarah, Scott's younger sister by five years, was a good student and, from all accounts, a normal child. Sarah was too young to come to the hospital and I never met her. Often her needs were secondary, with so much time being spent assuring Scott had the care he needed. Sarah's hurt feelings were becoming an issue and the family (without Scott) was being treated in family therapy by a social worker.

By trade, Teddy was a salesman, having tried his hand at selling everything from cars to liquor in the local corner store. Because of high medical costs and years of inconsistent work, Teddy struggled to pay the bills. The Polinski's lived in a small apartment and most of their free time was spent at the hospital or trying to contact a new doctor. Many team members felt the family would be better served if more time were spent with Sarah and less with Scott. In the team's opinion, the Polinski parents had sacrificed much and needed to care for themselves and their daughter. Perhaps this was true. At the time, I reserved judgment being new to the field and relatively inexperienced.

As is the way of life, I eventually left that job and did not see Scott, Helen or Teddy again for many years. One day, on the way home from work, I stopped for take-out food and ran into the Polinskis having lunch.

It turned out that, because of newer, advanced medications for schizophrenia, Scott was well enough to go on outings. After lunch, Teddy said they were bringing Scott back to the hospital; I couldn't help but notice Sarah was not with them.

I sat for a moment and chatted with the Polinski family. Speaking with each, I observed the effects of time and age. Scott's face had grown haggard and he was slowly eating a piece of chicken. He looked burnt out; the schizophrenia was running its course. Helen, who didn't seem to be her "energetic self," smiled at me. At the time, I wondered if she remembered who I was. Teddy was the one who did most of the talking. After 10 minutes of news about the hospital, I excused myself, picked-up an order of chicken and said goodbye.

As I walked to the parking lot, I recalled thinking how sad was their lot in life. I wondered, for a moment, how I would have handled the same hand. Then I got into my car, forgot about their problems and drove home.

Of course, there would be nothing more to the story if I did not again cross paths with the Polinski family.

A few months later, I stopped at the same take-out place and as I walked toward the counter to order, I saw Teddy sitting at a table, alone, nursing a cup of coffee. Slowly, I walked up to Teddy and asked, "How are you doing?" I must have startled him and, for a few seconds Teddy stared as if he did not recognize me. Finally, he spoke, "You're from the hospital and used to work with Scott, right?"

"Yes, I am. Where are Scott and Helen? Do you all still come here for lunch?"

Sadly, Teddy replied, "Not today." It was at this point I pulled-up a chair and began to listen.

Over the ensuing weeks and months, Teddy and I became good friends. We met many times to share a cup of coffee. Gradually, I learned more about his family. At the time, I did not realize their story would become my own. For you see, no one is spared the cup of suffering and illness. This is the human condition.

I share Teddy's story because how he struggled and found lasting happiness serves as an example and belongs to us all.

II – Scott

It was early morning and Teddy rested at the edge of the bed. He awoke before the alarm and struggled to get his thoughts together. During the night, he had gotten up four times to piss. The combination of urinary pressure and a reoccurring dream made for an uncomfortable night. Now he was tired and the day was just beginning. Teddy grumbled getting old sucked… and that damn dream. It kept coming back. What did it mean? When he had previously spoken to his family doctor about it, the simple reply was, "When you are ready, you will understand its meaning."

Well, no time to think about that now, he thought, I need to get to the hospital.

Teddy sat in the front of the bus with the other old men and women. As he stared out the window, he saw his reflection and began to think about Helen. Together they had ridden this bus many times. Together they had seen Teddy' hair thin and gradually fall out. Helen used to say that the gray hair and bald spot on the top of his head made him look distinguished. Each time she repeated it, Teddy smiled but he never felt distinguished. All Teddy ever felt was fatigue and annoyance. It took him years to understand and get past the anger. He was angry at life and all the heartache. It was so late in the game and he was beginning to enjoy himself again. Then Helen got sick. Teddy figured some people were born under an unlucky star.

Continuing to gaze out the bus window at the houses on Eastchester Road, Teddy pondered the dream. That damn dream. He wondered what it meant. Every few nights, why did it keep coming back?

Teddy was 17 years old and it was 11:30 p.m. on the last day of summer vacation. It was a hot, balmy night and Teddy could smell the ocean and salt mist. Tomorrow everyone was going back to his or her life in the city. The freedom of swimming in the surf, meeting new girls, and riding the roller coaster at Paradise Land would be over until next year. Yet, Teddy knew for him there was no next year. He felt it.

As Teddy stood looking through the chain link fence, at the closed amusement park, he longed for one last swim in the fresh water of the swimming pool. This pool was his favorite spot. He liked the ocean surf, but the cool, clean water of the pool had a calming, yet invigorating effect. When Teddy came out of the water, he felt renewed like a new person. After a swim, he was happy and alive. Ready to face whatever lay ahead.

No one was around. Teddy was the only person there. Tomorrow, they would drain the pool, cover it, and close it for the winter. Just like the coaster and other rides, the pool would be shut down for the season. How Teddy longed to go swimming. It would be easy to climb the fence; it was chain link and eight feet high. In a matter of seconds, he could be over the top.

Yet, Teddy froze. He imagined the water as it cooled and refreshed him. And as he stood, unable to move, the truly frightening part was that Teddy realized this was his last chance to go swimming. He had a premonition; beginning tomorrow, his life would change. Events would dictate that he would never return to Paradise Land and go for a swim in the cool, clean, fresh water.

Teddy felt his heart beat faster and sweat form on his face. What should he do? The pool was less than twenty feet from where he stood. Should he take a chance, climb the fence and break the rules? The amusement park and street were deserted. He could be in the pool in seconds. Teddy stood there unable to decide.

This was the reoccurring dream. Over the last six months, he had this dream many times. It was always the same. Teddy froze. He could not decide what to do? Finally, the anxiety built and he awoke panicked in a full sweat.

The ride from Coop City to the state hospital took about twenty-five minutes. Then, the walk from the bus stop to the Main Building took another fifteen minutes or so. Teddy was a slow walker. On sunny, warm days, like this one, the walk was spent clearing his mind and fortifying his nerves for what he would find inside.

Over the many years he had been visiting Scott, Teddy never got used to the suffering he encountered. So many lives confused, lost and pained. Truly, the mind was a world few understood. When it was plagued by voices, hallucinations, fear and distrust, many times the person never regained their balance. Often this degree of psychological turmoil had a lasting effect and those discharged were never the same.

Teddy walked across the field and thought about his son. Scott, in years of treatment, had never reached the point where he could be trusted to live on the outside. Even to this day, very little of what Scott said made sense and he could not hold a conversation for very long. Their visits were often filled with hand and foot rituals that Scott performed to protect the world from his anger.

Now in his early forties, Scott's hair was gray and had begun to recede, his former thin frame thickened with a growing mid-section. Not enough exercise the doctor's claimed. My God, Teddy thought, it would be a miracle if Scott could exercise or do anything for five minutes at a time.

The psychiatrists explained Scott's condition as an organic deterioration of the brain. Over time this would grow progressively worse, and Scott would begin to forget simple things like tying his shoes. The present course of treatment was directed at symptoms, not the disease process itself. Medicine helped reduce anxiety and slow the process, but not cure or correct it.

It was difficult to accept his only son was loony tunes and may have inherited the crazy gene from his family. Both Helen and Teddy discussed this with the doctors and their advice was not to blame themselves for something they could not control. The doctors maintained that no one knew the cause of schizophrenia or organic brain syndrome. A number of theories were proposed and most authorities felt these illnesses came about as the result of a chemical imbalance. Medication that was prescribed acted upon the brain's chemistry to bring about a temporary reduction of symptoms. Researchers hoped that someday, they could isolate the genes that produced these diseases and cure it.

All Teddy knew was that one day he had a normal son, someone who liked to get-up in the morning and go to school and the next day Scott was afraid to leave his room. Scott said the other children were laughing and making fun of him; he could hear them in his head. This started in the first grade. At one point, things got so bad Scott would not leave his room and refused to eat.

School officials came to the apartment and they were not able to reason with Scott. He grew angry, stating he was afraid and was not leaving his room to go to school. All Scott wanted to do was curl-up on his bed and hide beneath the covers. He did not know why the students were making fun of him; he never did anything to hurt them.

After a few days, Scott was taken out of his room by a team of mental health professionals and brought to the nearby state children's hospital. From that day, Scott was a ward of the state, spending the majority of his life in institutions. There were brief periods when Scott was at home, but these were spent hiding in his room.

Over the years, many doctors worked with Scott.

At 11 a.m., as Teddy approached the steps to the Main Building, he saw Pedro out front smoking a cigarette. Pedro was a patient on Scott's ward and waited for Teddy and Helen's visit each Saturday. Pedro had no family and attached himself to the Polinskis. Pedro came to America when Castro let the 'Cuban boat people' leave and, after a couple of years living on the streets of New York City, wound up in a state psychiatric hospital. Pedro wore a full, brown beard with long, uncombed hair that reached his shoulders. In his late 50s, with a large, round belly and friendly smile, often he could be observed talking to people no one else could see.

Unlike Scott, Pedro had grounds privileges and waited faithfully for the Polinskis to arrive. Teddy and Helen brought enough food, coffee and cigarettes for Pedro and some of the others. Patients had little money to buy personal items for themselves.

When Pedro saw Teddy, he called out, "Pappy, Pappy, you are here. You are here, but where is Mammy? Mammy, she no come? She no come?"

Teddy prepared himself for this question and wanted to talk about it as little as possible. Gently, as he had done each Saturday for months, he replied to Pedro, "No, Helen could not come, but she made sure you got your coffee and cigarettes. Mammy said, 'Make sure you bring Pedro his coffee and cigarettes."

Pedro looked sad and thought about Helen for a moment, but then smiled. "I miss Mammy, I miss her . . . Can I have coffee now?"

Teddy patted Pedro on the shoulder and replied, "when we get upstairs on the ward. Coffee, when we get upstairs on the ward."

Then, Teddy and Pedro walked together into the Main Building, through the lobby, to the elevators.

As Teddy approached the elevators, he considered the many trips to this place. Over the years little seemed to have changed. Sure, the place was cleaner and fewer patients were sitting idly about. Advances in psychotropic drugs and advocacy groups helped thousands get discharged. But it was still an institution and you could feel the misery in the walls.

Recently, the lobby was repainted and new furniture purchased but somehow it still looked stark. This time there were no patients begging for cigarettes and coffee. It still happened on the ward, but Helen and Teddy always brought enough; it was the least they could do.

For a few moments, the coffee and cigarettes brought pleasure and interrupted the monotony of the day. Teddy noticed that patients willingly shared what little they had, saving a sip of coffee or a puff on their cigarette for one of their mates.

Riding the elevator to the fourth floor, Teddy felt the butterflies in his stomach. You would think, after all these years, he would not be nervous visiting the ward. But Teddy never knew what he would find when he walked through the doors. Would one of the patients be screaming and cursing at the top of their lungs? Or would he be greeted by a naked gent who just disrobed in the hallway because his 'clothes were on fire'?

While Teddy rang the bell, Pedro and he waited. Teddy listened for footsteps, or even patients talking, behind the solid metal door. When the door opened, patients sometimes tried to run out and escape; when entering from the hall you always had to be on your guard.

As Teddy rang again, he wondered what was taking the staff so long to unlock the door. It was 11:15 a.m. and Teddy knew that Scott was getting anxious. Teddy was late and Scott was probably pacing the halls, clapping his hands, protecting the world from his growing wrath. Teddy brought a cheeseburger and fries from the Coop City

Diner. When Scott was well enough, this was one of the places they went for lunch.

Finally, a female staff member opened the door to the ward. She apologized for taking so long, explaining she had been busy with a load of laundry and the others were setting up lunch for the patients. Quickly, before anyone could run out, Teddy and Pedro entered and walked toward the visitor's room. The visitor's room was located on the left, down the hall fifteen feet or so from the front door. They could see Scott; he was already waiting inside. It was lunchtime and the other patients were slowly walking down the hall toward the dining room.

After Teddy signed the visitor's log, he and Pedro sat beside Scott on a sofa in the middle of the room. All the while, Scott was calling out, "Did you bring it? Did you bring it?" Softly Teddy replied, as he placed food on the table in front of Scott, "I brought a cheeseburger and fries, with plenty of ketchup, just like you like it." Hurriedly, Scott was tearing into the paper, which covered the plate unable to wait any longer.

Teddy thought to himself, as he watched his son take fast, large bites, if you met Scott on the street, you might think he looked like any other sloppily dressed, middle-aged man. Until you took a second, harder look, then you would notice he was not well.

Scott was forty-two years old, but around the eyes looked much older. The eyes were the windows to the soul; they showed the years of inner torment. When you looked into Scott's eyes, you saw pain and anguish. His hollow, blank stare called out to rest.

Scott's hair matched the gray stubble on his face; he had not been shaved today. While seated it was difficult to tell how tall he was but Teddy knew. They were both the same height, 5'4", and over the past year Scott had gained more weight. He must be over 220 pounds, Teddy thought.

As Scott ate, he said nothing and made no eye contact; this was the way lunch usually went. Every few seconds, Scott's head would twitch from side to side. This involuntary movement made eating a challenge, with food falling on Scott's white T-shirt and brown, elastic-waist pants. Teddy remembered, for safety reasons, patients were not allowed to wear belts. The doctors said Scott's head movement was a side effect of the medication and had a name for it, which Teddy could not pronounce.

After gulping down only part of his burger and fries, without a word, Scott got up, stood in the doorway and began a sequence of handclaps. Sometimes a rocking motion accompanied the claps, which were always in an organized pattern. Today, Scott rocked and clapped in groups of three. He did this four times before turning around twice and repeated the same sequence of claps. After 30 seconds, he moved on to the dining room doorway and performed the same ritual. It was not unusual for Scott to clap from doorway to doorway for hours.

The doctor's believed this was Scott's way of protecting the world. In Scott's mind, he was evil and so powerful that if he did not perform these rituals, the world would be unprotected from his fury. In fact, the staff used this behavior as a predictor of violence. If Scott did not perform the door ritual, staff knew he was upset and would eventually strike out.

Quietly, Teddy and Pedro watched as Scott slowly made his way down the hall. When Scott was out of sight, Teddy opened a bag of cookies and offered some to Pedro. Pedro waited anxiously, but gratefully accepted the sugar cookies.

By this time, some of the other patients finished lunch. They found their way into the lounge and were asking for cookies. Mrs. Adams, the heavy, middle-aged attendant who let Teddy and Pedro onto the ward, supervised things and said, "Okay, but only two cookies each."

As Teddy gave out the sugar cookies to the other patients, he took deep calming breaths. Sadly, he thought, it was always the same. These poor people were enjoying the simplest of things. They never seemed to get enough food. They had just eaten and still they were hungry. Teddy wondered if medication makes them this way, or if the food was a substitute for things in life they missed.

Teddy gazed about the visitor's lounge, searching for Helen. He missed her. Across the years, there were many discussions with staff and meals shared; the hospital had been a big part of their lives.

By now, Pedro was helping himself to the left over burger and fries and Teddy stood to look out the window. The higher up in the hospital you went, the better the view; also, the longer the stay. The patients on the lower floors were the first prepared for discharge. Nowadays, the floors above were sealed and their floor, the fourth, was the end of the line. From here, you could see their apartment in Coop City; over the years, the hospital had cast a long shadow.

In the early years, when Scott was first hospitalized, Teddy needed a 'sounding board' for his frustration. One day, Teddy wanted to give the Rabbi, as a representative of God, a good piece of his mind. Teddy found his way to the chaplaincy and, because the Rabbi worked part-time, only the Protestant Reverend was available. Over time, Teddy and the Reverend became close friends.

Reverend Wilson worked full-time at the hospital and had a small congregation at a church in the south Bronx. Wilson was an intelligent, caring person who Teddy instantly liked. Wilson was down to earth and ready to take on patient and family member's doubts about the mercy of God and the goodness of life.

When Teddy first experienced the despair and madness of the state psychiatric hospital, he was distraught and full of angry questions. "If God is loving and cares about us, why did God make people so sick and crazy? Look around at these unfortunates, how does this madness make any sense? And what of the parents of these poor people, cursing the day they brought their own children into the world?"

Wilson, with gentle, caring eyes, looked at Teddy and softly replied, "No one knows the answer to these questions. Truly, that is the province of God. He is all loving and knows what each person needs. You must have faith and trust God."

Teddy was furious. He hesitated for a moment, before saying, in a raised voice, "When I first met you, I thought you might be different."

"What do you mean?" questioned Wilson.

"That's the same line, the same easy answer I've heard since Scott got sick. The psychiatrists explain Scott's illness as a problem within the brain's chemistry and offer hope, 'it is just a matter of time until a cure is discovered.' The clergy explain it as the will of God and to have faith in some inexplicable reason for all of this. Let me tell you something, that's not enough! When someone in your family, who you love as part of yourself, comes down with a life changing illness like schizophrenia, it rips your heart out. You want something more.

You want an answer as to why you are going through this and you want a cure. Can you understand that?"

"Yes, I think I can. Let me tell you something about myself and how I came to my own answers about all of this."

"You mean it's not the will of God?"

"Please, give me a chance. Let me tell you about it in my own way. I have been a clergyman for nearly thirty years and have seen people in good times and bad. I asked the same question as you; how could God create such madness? I too wanted more than the standard answer.

"Well, it wasn't until a member of my own family was stricken with paranoid schizophrenia that I pushed for an answer. Yes, I saw the torment and hopelessness and I prayed. My answer was a long time coming."

"Are you going to tell me?"

"Be patient, let me tell the story. One day, I was attending a lecture where a Buddhist Monk spoke to this point. It seemed, from their point of view, certain souls chose to be born into a life of infirmity so that others might benefit. They took on the mantle of sickness so their soul might learn and others around them advance. Illness, to these Monks, was a vehicle whereby all could reach upward.

"From their point of view, life was an opportunity to grow spiritually and sickness was a great teacher. Over the years, I have considered this a possibility."

"But that makes no sense. You mean Scott chose to be schizophrenic so Helen and I could benefit. Please, that explanation seems as flawed as the one about having faith. Besides, I don't even believe in reincarnation."

"Think about it. Give it time. On one level, if there were no patients in the hospital, many of us would not be here. Scott's illness provides many with an opportunity to work, serve and question.

"If Scott never became ill, would you search for an answer to your questions? If there were no pain or death, would you push yourself to understand the meaning of life? Affliction is a burning that pushes us to question."

Scott returned to the visitor's room, stood beside the table and helped Pedro finish the sugar cookies and milk. Then he went to the bathroom door, which was part of the visitor's room, and continued his ritualistic clapping. First, he bent over, faced the bathroom door and clapped hands 4 times against his thighs. Then he turned around twice, bent over again, and repeated the clapping motions.

After he completed this set, Scott walked to the door of the visitor's room and repeated the movements. While Scott was busy clapping, Teddy called out to Mrs. Adams, who was finishing up lunch, "Is it alright if I take Scott and Pedro for a walk on the hospital grounds? Did the doctor leave permission?"

Mrs. Adams called back, "Yeah, it's alright. He wrote it down in the order book. I left Scott's hat and sunscreen for you in the utility room. Remember, get both of them back by 1 o'clock medication. If Scott gives you any trouble call up to the ward. When you're ready I'll unlock the door."

"OK, but I don't think there will be any problems."

Scott, Pedro and Teddy were outside the Main Building walking around on the large lawn. For the most part, the grounds were deserted. Most of the patients were on their ward, finishing lunch and waiting for medication. Few visitors arrived this early; regular visiting hours were 2- 8 p.m. daily. Teddy came early because it was easier this way. Feeding Scott lunch gave Teddy something to do. Scott rarely spoke and, over the years, there was less and less to talk about. Confined to the hospital, Scott was removed from the world of family, friends and events. Scott never asked about these things.

Suddenly, Scott began to walk faster. Teddy and Pedro had trouble keeping up. Teddy realized Scott had seen something and followed behind. Then, before Teddy could do anything, Scott was beside an outdoor garbage can and picking through its contents. As Teddy approached, he called out, "Scott stop. You just ate. Leave it alone."

But Scott ignored his father. Hurriedly, he was opening some aluminum foil, picking out the remains of barbecue chicken and swallowing as fast as he could.

Sadly, Teddy turned to Pedro and said, "Go back to the lobby and call up to the ward. We need help. Pedro, you know the ward extension right?"

Pedro replied, "Yes Pappy." Then he ran back to the lobby to call the ward.

Teddy knew it was useless to try and take the garbage away from Scott; he would strike back. When Scott had first done this, the three of them were together. Helen, Scott and Teddy were enjoying a quiet picnic on the hospital grounds. Scott had more than enough to eat. Suddenly, he got-up from the table and began rummaging through a nearby garbage can. As he found something, Scott put it in his mouth and ate it. Frantically, Helen yelled at Scott, "Stop it! Stop it!" This did no good and Helen needed Teddy to do something. So, Teddy tried to pull the garbage out of Scott's hand. Scott resisted and punched Teddy on the shoulder. Then, Scott ran away with the garbage.

This upset Helen even more and she began to sob. Finally, after 30 minutes of searching, the staff caught up with Scott near Pelham Parkway. He was hiding in the bushes, eating garbage, by the fence that surrounded the hospital grounds.

Since that time, Scott exhibited this behavior sporadically. It was impossible to tell when he would do it again. Sometimes, the visits went well and other times, like this, Scott cut the visit short by eating garbage.

By now, Mrs. Adams and a male coworker arrived. Immediately, Scott placed the garbage in a nearby can. Then the staff each took one of Scott's arms and escorted him back to the ward. Pedro was trailing behind and called, "Bye Pappy."

As they walked toward the Main Building, Teddy sat on a bench and watched. He wondered why Scott heeded the ward staff but ignored his own father? Slowly, a tear fell from Teddy's right eye and he took a deep, long breath and sighed.

After a time, Teddy pulled himself together. Finally, the hurt passed. He looked up at the sky and watched the moving clouds, focusing on their changing pattern and thought about his old friend, Reverend Wilson. How he missed their discussions, their closeness.

Teddy never considered himself a religious man. Over the years, he had little need for God. Early on, Teddy decided God was not doing that good of a job, and it made little sense to rely on someone who made as many mistakes as the average person did. In fact, Teddy felt that if he were God's boss, God would have been canned long ago.

During weekly visits to the hospital, Teddy and Reverend Wilson grew closer. What an odd combination, with him, a White Jew from Coop City, and Wilson, a Black Protestant Reverend from the South Bronx. Often Teddy wondered what they had in common. Yet, they were drawn to each other and Teddy enjoyed their talks. He could say whatever he wanted to Reverend Wilson and never worried about offending. In time, their relationship and discussions extended beyond the confines of the state hospital and Wilson's role as minister to the hospital community.

Often, Teddy would leave Helen and Scott to go speak with Wilson in his office. These visits gave him a respite, a safe place, even if for a few minutes. He remembered another time they discussed illness.

Teddy questioned, "In the Bible it says something to the effect that those God Loves, he tests with afflictions. Is this not so?"

Wilson replied, "Yes, I believe the Bible makes that reference."

"Well, what kind of Father wants affliction for his children? When you walk around and see the madness here, how can it be justified? Only a cruel Father wants his children tormented by voices and persecutory delusions."

"Teddy, the answer to your question cannot be understood by the mind. The mind questions and wonders what kind of God would do this to his children. The heart must answer. What the mind asks, the heart reveals. The answer to this question must be perceived and felt."

"What do you mean, perceived and felt? Is that another way to avoid answering the question?"

"No. Some things cannot be thought out like an algebra or math equation. The mind, or consciousness, has many levels and capacities. Every day the mind questions…what kind of God creates incurable madness? The higher consciousness, or soul, replies. The mind pushes. But the heart must answer this inquiry."

"Sounds like religious mumbo-jumbo to me. It doesn't matter what the religious training is, the difficult answers are always the same. 'Have faith.' 'Pray.' 'As God Wills, you will find the answers.' When I see Scott lost in the haze of voices, unable to feed himself, and Helen trying to tend his needs, I want an answer, not platitudes."

Reverend Wilson looked fondly at Teddy for a moment, as if he was considering what next to say. Pushing a little harder, he queried, "Teddy, when was the last time you prayed?"

Incredulously, Teddy stared at Wilson and replied, "Aren't you listening to me? Why would I pray to a God I don't respect or understand?"

"Because that's how you get the answer. You talk to God and speak like you are speaking to me. Why is my son unable to care for himself? Why does he have schizophrenia and in a place like this? Teddy, God loves you and has placed this in your path so you may know Him."

Teddy stood and began walking toward the door. "You know, John, sometimes you talk such bullshit I can barely keep my temper. That stuff about getting to know God better is just plain shit. It's crap the clergy tosses at you to confuse you and control your mind."

Outside, in front of the Main Building, Teddy sat on a bench watching the cars go up and down the highway. Teddy thought, "The people in those cars seem to have purpose and direction, hurrying to get someplace. I wonder if they are going to visit someone who is not feeling well. In a psychiatric hospital, perhaps? Probably not."

God, he needed a sympathetic ear. Slowly these visits were killing him. Oh, that he had John Wilson to listen. What a kind and sympathetic friend John had been. Sadly, it was four years since John passed, when throat cancer proved too strong a foe. There were treatments, but they did not work. It seemed even God's employees got the short end of things.

As Teddy stood, stretching out his arms, he gazed at the summer sun and began to smile. Taking a long, deep, slow breath brought the smell of onion grass and wild flowers. Their fragrance reminded him of John and how he loved to open the windows to his office and smell the flowers. And thinking of John helped Teddy feel better; for an instant, it was almost like being with him.

Teddy turned and began walking back toward the bus stop on Eastchester Road.

It was a beautiful day and Teddy decided to extend his walk. He could catch the bus on Pelham Parkway and stretch his legs for another twenty minutes or so.

Walking along Eastchester Road, feeling the sun at his back, Teddy wondered about his life. Certainly, he had never meant it to turn out this way, going from the psychiatric hospital to the nursing home. First Scott, then visit Helen. On off days, when he did not visit, it was going from the apartment to work in the liquor store.

At the end of things, Teddy hoped he and Helen could spend time together in the sun. They spoke about going south for winters and keeping the apartment in Coop City to be close to Scott. Many of their friends moved to Florida and it would not be difficult to find an economy apartment for two months. There were plenty of people to assist them.

In their plans, if the liquor store did not give him time off each year, he would find another job. There were always jobs for good salesmen and he was plenty good. Most people did not realize the secret to sales was taking an interest in the person who was buying. Once the buyer felt the salesperson was interested in helping meet their needs, the sales were just about made.

While it was true that at the liquor store Teddy did not get to use the full range of his skills, he was still the best salesperson in the place and Fred, the boss, knew it. In the Coop City store, people were generally in a hurry and knew what they wanted. The pitch was about the selection, the quality of product, for the price. To know the quality of products, you had to do your homework and read about production.

Teddy hated to read and, over the last couple of years, got along on 'bullshit' and a smile. For an instant, Teddy felt guilty about being lazy and not caring what he told people, then reassured himself, "What the hell. It's only a job. It pays some of the bills and gives me an opportunity to be around other people."

Continuing along Eastchester Road, Teddy worked up a sweat. Walking past the City Hospital, he was nearing Pelham Parkway and the next bus stop. Seeing an ambulance pull up to the Emergency Room door, he wondered aloud, "So many people coming and going.

Life and death all around and rarely do we give death a second thought until it's our time or the time of a loved one."

Just as Teddy was getting ready to cross Pelham Parkway and catch the bus to White Plains Road, a street person came up to Teddy and questioned, "Change? Can you spare some change?"

Teddy hated street people, particularly when they begged for money. Most of them, like this fellow, looked healthy enough to work. He could not have been more than thirty years old, a little scruffy and dirty perhaps, but healthy enough to work. Teddy wondered why he should give any money. The money was probably going for drugs not for food. You never saw any overweight street people.

Helen was kinder than Teddy; she always gave something. Teddy worked too hard for his money, and where did all of Helen's kindness get her? In a nursing home, that's where her kindness got her.

Again, the homeless fellow inquired, "Change? Can you spare some change?"

For an instant, lost in his thoughts, Teddy forgot the fellow was there. Regaining his senses, he answered, "No."

Instead of leaving, the homeless fellow stood there with his hand out. This surprised Teddy. Usually after Teddy said "no," the homeless person walked away.

Getting angry, Teddy inquired, "What do you want? I said, no change."

The young homeless man smiled and extended his hand further. He said, "Take it. If you have nothing for me, I have something for you."

Seeing nothing in the fellow's hand, Teddy replied, "I see nothing. Take what? You have nothing in your hand."

Continuing to smile, the toothless fellow said, "The opportunity, take the opportunity. Remember the dream?"

For an instant, Teddy was startled. When he regained his composure, Teddy wanted to question the fellow. Teddy wondered, perhaps for some change, if the fellow would tell him the meaning of his dream.

Quickly, Teddy gave the fellow a handful of coins and said, "Now, tell me about my dream."

Walking away, the young man said, "Old man, what dream? I don't know what you are talking about."

Unable to speak, Teddy wondered if he was losing his mind and imagined the homeless fellow spoke about his dream.

III – Helen

Teddy had switched from the Pelham Parkway to the White Plains Road bus and was seated in the front, next to the driver. In the rear, he could hear a group of teenage boys and girls laughing, shouting and singing along to their boom box. Teddy wondered, why did they play their music so loud and what did they have to be so happy about? It was years since he was that happy and carefree. It was the summer he had the season pass to Paradise Land. That was a long, long time ago and a summer he could not forget.

As the bus wound its way toward the north Bronx and the White Plains Nursing Home on 233rd street, Teddy was growing nervous. When he visited Helen, he never knew what he would find. At least with Scott the visits were more or less the same. It was just a matter of time before the illness took over and Scott did something that required a return to the ward. Even when they went to Yonkers for take-out, Scott eventually did something that demonstrated his inability to live on the outside.

With Helen, the course of the illness was unpredictable. Some days when Teddy visited, Helen was as clear as a sunny, summer day. During these moments, Teddy wondered if she were well enough to go home, to the apartment, for a visit. Helen remembered his name, that they were married, and had two children. She even called the children by name and inquired after each. Teddy told her about Scott, their neighbors in Coop City, and did his best to avoid details concerning Sarah. Old feelings of hurt between mother and daughter ran deep and Teddy wanted to avoid upsetting Helen. It had been a year since mother and daughter spoke.

On other days, Helen sat perfectly still and did not acknowledge Teddy. Looking past him when he spoke, Helen would not recognize him. Many times she thought he worked in the nursing home.

Those were the really difficult, gut wrenching visits. None of the former, lively Helen was present. It was like he was talking to an empty shell. He knew she was still in there someplace, but to what lonely, dark corner had she retreated? He knew he could not protect her from herself and, as he thought about her alone and hiding, it brought a pain to his heart. Oh, what a cruel illness to allow moments of clarity, then no recognition of their former life.

So much about the mind that doctors did not understand. Now, two members of his family were lost in the mysterious haze of the mind.

Getting off the bus and walking the few blocks from the bus stop to the nursing home, it was mid-afternoon and sunny. Teddy wondered if, perhaps some of the residents were outside enjoying the warm day.

Teddy drew closer to the home and noticed an elderly, black gentleman walking toward him. As the fellow approached, Teddy began to feel uneasy. Something about that man was familiar. My God, Teddy thought, it's John Wilson. It can't be; John died four years ago. Moreover, as the fellow walked beside Teddy, he realized it wasn't John. The fellow barely resembled his old friend.

Teddy continued walking and breathed a long sigh of relief. He mumbled to himself, that's the second time today my mind has played a trick. First, it was with a homeless fellow, now I'm seeing deceased friends. I wonder if I'm going crazy like Scott and Helen. Teddy grew frightened; his heart beat faster, sweat formed on his forehead and he started to shake. Somehow, he forced himself to keep walking and concentrate on where he was going.

Nearing the nursing home, Teddy observed a group of residents sitting outside in wheelchairs beneath the shaded awning in front. The afternoon was sunny and temperatures were in the low 80s. Teddy knew that if Helen were feeling well, she would be outdoors enjoying the street activity and watching passing cars. At one time, she had an active, inquisitive mind and enjoyed being with people. Now, with the deterioration, it was difficult to tell what she liked; she was unstable and forgotten much of her life.

At one time, their apartment was full of plants, flowers and cuttings. Helen liked watching things grow and tending plants back to health. She was kind and loving.

Teddy approached the home and saw Helen outside. As he grew closer, Teddy called out her name and Helen responded by turning her head to see who was calling. This was a good sign, Teddy thought; at least she recognizes her name.

The female attendant who was supervising also turned to see who was approaching. Instantly, she recognized Teddy and called, "Hello Mr. Polinski. It's a beautiful day today."

"Sure is Matilda and it's good to see you," Teddy replied.

"Mrs. Polinski is having a good day so we brought her outside to wait for you. Was that alright?"

"Thanks Matilda. I'm happy she is feeling well. We'll go for a short walk, if you don't mind, around back." Teddy bent over and kissed Helen on the cheek. Next, he turned the wheelchair and began pushing toward the rear of the home where there were benches. All the while, Helen sat quietly not saying a word.

After a few minutes, Teddy and Helen were comfortable. Helen was enjoying the sucking candy that Teddy brought her and they rested peacefully in the shade behind the home. Helen was in her wheelchair and Teddy was alongside on one of the benches. Teddy and Helen had been married for almost 40 years and they could sit quietly, without a word, enjoying each other's company for hours. But today Helen had something to say.

"Teddy, how long have I been in this place? I know you told me, but I can't remember."

Smiling, for Teddy had told Helen many times, he replied, "About six months. Why do you ask?"

"Well, I wonder, when will I be going home, back to our apartment? It must be terribly lonely for you and I miss being in my own apartment."

Teddy realized, in all likelihood, Helen would never be going back to their apartment, unless a cure was discovered in the next few months. This was highly unlikely. After this time, the degeneration will have advanced to the point that, even if a cure were discovered, her brain could not be restored. There was no point in hurting Helen, and Teddy knew she would forget what he said. So, Teddy was hopeful.

"Last time I spoke to the doctor, he said you were making progress and would be going home for a visit soon."

"Oh, that's good news. When will that be?"

"In a few weeks."

Helen smiled and they sat quietly. Then, Helen spoke again. "How is Scott? When was the last time you saw him?"

Teddy paused, looked kindly into Helen's eyes and replied, "I visited Scott just before coming to see you. He is much the same and said to give you a kiss." Then, Teddy bent over and kissed Helen lightly on the cheek.

She smiled and said, "He is such a good boy. When can I see him?"

Calmly, Teddy answered, "I spoke to Scott's doctor who said that when you come to the apartment, Scott can visit. They will work out the arrangements. I hope you will like that?"

"Oh, Teddy, of course I will. Why wouldn't I like that?"

After a little more time of sitting quietly, in each other's company, Teddy observed the glazed-over expression take hold of Helen's face. Her facial features froze and she had a far away look in her eyes. The only motion, on her face, was the blinking of her eyes.

Teddy realized that Helen had slipped into that place where there was no hint of her identity. This was a place where the old Helen no longer existed. Gone were the memories of self and family.

This was the thing that hurt the most. Somehow, Teddy had survived the years of illness with Scott, and the distance his sickness had created between their daughter, Sarah, and them. While this hurt deeply, at least Helen and Teddy faced it together. Now, Teddy's friend and companion were gone and her absence left a terrible emptiness inside.

Alone, Teddy faced the demons in his own mind. Why was he created to watch those he loved go mad?

Helen spoke, returning from that distant place. Looking at Teddy, she said, "Mister, I am getting cold. Can you wheel me inside?"

Slowly, Teddy stood and gently grabbed hold of the wheelchair and began pushing Helen back to the front of the nursing home.

As Teddy exited the bus, in front of the shopping center in Coop City, he shook his head and mumbled as he walked, "This day has been almost too much to bear. First visiting my son, who has been lost in his mind for most of his life, and now my wife, who has been lost for nearly six months.

"Somehow I looked forward, after all the work was done, to retiring with my beloved Helen. This kept me going. Like so many others, together we would go south and spend our remaining days in the sun and visit the senior center. Now I am alone. What kind of God does this to people? Surely, Scott never hurt anyone. His illness came on just as he was entering school; he was barely alive long enough to comb his own hair when it struck. What was his sin that he was punished so?

"And Helen. What was her sin that God should strike her? I have never known as kind and loving a person."

Riding up the elevator to his apartment on the 24th floor, Teddy kept trying to think of a reason why a loving God would do this to people, particularly kind and loving people. When Teddy and Reverend Wilson had their conversations about this, Teddy had not understood nor accepted any answer. Over the years, little had changed and Teddy found himself mentally going over their talks, hoping to discover something he had missed.

John had said, many times, "Each person must find the meaning to their pain. This meaning is on an inner level. It is not something the rational mind understands. The rational mind was created to ask the question and the heart, or inner wisdom, provides an answer. The answer must be perceived, not thought out."

Each time John told him this, Teddy replied, "Again with evasive answers. Answers that cannot be challenged. John, you and I go around in circles; it is a little dance we do. Religion responds, you must have faith my son. And I respond, this is a way of avoiding and admitting there is no answer to the question, why do we get ill? How do we get past this?"

John always smiled at Teddy's capacity for a quick answer and his tenacity. "Teddy, the scriptures are clear as to the reason for illness and trials. The scriptures say when God loves someone, God hands them the cup of affliction and each person must drink of this cup.

"Now, the rational mind rebels at this answer. It cries out, how can a loving father do this to his child? Is this not a cruel way to learn the lesson, whatever the lesson might be? Isn't there a kinder way to present the material?"

By this time, Teddy had reached the 24th floor and the elevator opened. He was tired of the same old repeating tapes in his head, very tired. Teddy walked out of the elevator and unlocked the door to his apartment. Then, he sat down in his easy chair, alone in the dark with his thoughts.

Teddy rested, but his mind kept going over their conversations. One day he pressed John for a personal answer, something not out of the scriptures. At first, John was reluctant but finally gave in. "Alright, I will explain my experience by sharing my personal answer to the question of why God placed cancer in my throat. At first I was angry and hurt. I reasoned, after 30 years of working for God and helping tend God's flock, my reward was this terrible disease and agonizing treatments. 'How can this be?' I wondered. The scriptures were clear about this: illness brings you closer to God. These were empty words to me.

"Well, I prayed long and hard for an answer and, Teddy, you will not like the answer; but it gave me comfort. For with the answer, came the spiritual peace and love of God. It was a spiritual caress and my soul rejoiced in peace. When the worldly life is taken, there is the spiritual life and caress of God's Mercy. It is a sublime, spiritual peace.

"Yes, God loves us and creates infirmity so we might know God better. For with the tears, the life of the spirit fully awakens. Because the world is filled with physical wonders, we easily forget that the reason for this world is ultimately spiritual. The journey is spiritual and the physical world is to be enjoyed, as God's servants. The point of the creation is to sing God's praise. We must never forget the world was created to lead us to God.

"The tears of sorrow soften the heart so we may fully experience the spiritual caress of God's love and mercy. These tears set the soul free, so that we can soar unfettered by the chains of the worldly life. This was the spiritual gift given to me when I went to visit the cancer doctors and they advised me about my chances."

Teddy continued to listen carefully but remained unconvinced and John sensed this. John paused for a moment and carefully chose his words, "Teddy, you asked me to elaborate based upon my own personal experience. Hesitantly, I did this knowing my answer would not satisfy you because, until I experienced the answer myself, I could not fully embrace it. While I spent most of my life helping others that were in pain, it was not until I drank from this cup myself did I fully understand. The answer was spiritual. You see, everything is created to lead us to God. Some find God in the eyes of a newborn and others in the tears of sorrow. This is according to individual destiny and the plan for each. The answer to your question must be experienced spiritually, not thought out by the mind."

As Teddy sat in the darkness of his three room apartment on the 24th floor, he was tired. Very tired. He was tired of visiting sick family members. He was tired of trying to figure out the reason for his life. He just wanted to rest and be loved.

Slowly, very slowly, Teddy fell asleep in his favorite easy chair. As he slept, his conscious mind rested for a time, his soul danced across the night, free in the beauty of God's empyrean light. For, you see, when a door closes, another opens and we must listen and heed the many portions of ourselves.

That night, as Teddy's soul danced across the cosmic ceiling, it embraced its freedom and celebrated its kinship with all things. It was a child of the universe and would live on, having come into this plane to learn and serve.

The part that was bound to the earth still rested on the 24th floor, in one of the many apartments in Coop City. Yet, each evening the part that was eternal danced free across the evening sky. After a time, the soul re-entered Teddy's body, gloriously emanating its light to the physical portion of its being. Very slowly, Teddy's body began to drink the cosmic song and its own inner light. As Teddy's physical consciousness merged with the higher portion of him, he began to rest and found himself dreaming again. Gradually, Teddy's higher soul was sending a message to the portion that was tied to the earth. In time, the part that was unsure and in turmoil would embrace that part which was triumphant and eternal.

Again, Teddy found himself standing outside of Paradise Land. It was 11:30 p.m. and the amusement park was closed for the season. He longed to climb the fence that stood between him and the relaxing water of the swimming pool that tomorrow would be drained for the season.

The summer of fun, enjoying the rides, being with friends, and the pure, clean water of the pool was over. Yet, he held in his hand the season pass that allowed him to go inside as many times as he wanted. Technically, there was still 30 minutes left to the season.

It was dark and all he had to do was jump the fence and dive into the water. How he longed to do this one last time.

Instinctively, he realized that in the morning he would be going back to the city, and all that lay before him was a lifetime of work and toil. This was his moment. No one was around. Why was he afraid to jump the chain link fence and go for one last swim in Paradise Land?

Teddy was frozen. He was afraid he might get caught. He stood by the fence, looking at the water, longing for the freedom and soothing release it brought him.

IV – Sarah

It was morning and Teddy awoke at his usual 6 a.m. Again, he fell asleep and spent the entire night in his easy chair. Lately, the old chair was getting more action than his bed. Teddy actually preferred the chair. The bed was not as comfortable, or didn't feel the same, without Helen.

Sunday morning and all was quiet in the apartment. Teddy did not have to be at work until 1 p.m. The liquor store, where he worked part-time, wasn't allowed to open until then. Something about the "Blue Laws," whatever those were.

Teddy walked into the kitchen to make a cup of coffee. In the morning, he needed a 'jolt' to get started. Teddy thought about the dream, as he got the "Mr. Coffee" started. He figured the dream was a holdover from his youth, when he went to the shore with his family. He enjoyed the amusement park and the water. After that summer, things changed. He went to work and later took on the responsibility of a family.

Yet, Teddy felt there must be more to the dream. If the meaning were that simple it would not keep coming back. In addition, this was the only reoccurring dream he ever had and intuitively he figured that the meaning must be deep and hidden.

While Teddy waited for the coffee to brew, inside his stomach he felt the anxiety and fear begin to build. Lately, this anxiety was always present. He knew he carried anxiety about what would happen next and it had turned him into a bundle of nerves. Constantly he feared another painful episode.

In his time, he had seen heartache. Having a son who was in a mental hospital means phone calls, at all hours, notifying them Scott was injured or in a fight. There was a rule that family had to be notified each time there was an injury. Others were always picking on Scott. After a time he and Helen put in writing they did not wish to be notified each time. Teddy now learned about these incidents when he visited Scott.

Over the last year, as Helen's condition deteriorated, Teddy came home nervous, never knowing what he would find. Specifically, as

Helen's memory failed, Teddy came home to find food and water all over the kitchen floor. The coup de grace occurred when Helen nearly set the apartment on fire. She was boiling water on the stove for tea and, after the water evaporated, the pan caught on fire. Fortunately, Teddy arrived just in time to put out the fire. It was then that he realized Helen needed to go to a home. For months, he had denied that her brain was failing.

Oh, the fear Teddy lived with to postpone the inevitable. Bit by bit, those he loved were taken from him.

Teddy got up and poured himself a cup of coffee, before moving to the living room for a sit in his favorite chair.

Teddy began channel surfing through the different shows on Sunday morning television. First, he tried to watch the news, but it was depressing. Clip after clip showed people doing horrible things to each other. He wondered, what happened to the world? Why was it filled with so many selfish, brutal people? What happened to decency and kindness?

Then he watched, or tried to watch, several political commentary shows. Each show featured politicians who had solutions to problems affecting the nation. Teddy wondered what it was like to be confident and have solutions to problems that vexed so many others.

Teddy could not remember a time when he felt confident about anything. It had been a long time since life had not kicked his butt with illness, medical bills or family problems. Most times, he was grateful to make it through the day and felt like he was holding on by a thread. Lately he was beginning to wonder about that thread. Yesterday there were two instances where he totally misread what was going on. One, with the young street fellow and the second with the man who he thought looked like John Wilson. Teddy feared he was starting to unravel and they might have to make room for him in the psychiatric hospital.

Teddy remembered his mother saying, "When you have your health, you have everything." She was right. It had been years since his family was healthy. During that time, there was much unrest and worry.

Teddy flicked to the morning religious shows. Often he wished he could find the assurance of faith these morning preachers professed.

Teddy knew that many of them were charlatans and wanted your donation, yet others, like his old friend John, were genuine and wanted to share some of the peace they had found.

It had been years since he was at peace and not preoccupied with Scott, or now Helen, getting the right treatment. When he went to visit, he feared the treatments were not working and that it would cost more money. These considerations filled his mind.

Religion could provide comfort, as John found, but Teddy could never get past the hurt. He was angry with God for striking those he loved. Teddy saw illness ripping his life apart as he lost Scott and Helen and Sarah.

As a result of Scott's illness, Sarah had been the one who hurt the most. All their time was spent on Scott and so little with Sarah. Many nights, Sarah needed help with her homework and Teddy was too tired to provide it. Working long hours and helping Helen get treatment for Scott, left Sarah alone.

In spite of it all, Sarah did well in school, raised her own family and tried not to resent the time and energy spent on Scott. Early on, the Polinski family went to counseling and, until recently, the sessions seemed to have benefited Sarah. Just before Helen's illness, when they visited Sarah's home in Long Island, one of Sarah's little ones needed attention and Helen, the concerned grandmother, tried to intervene. This 'meddling,' as Sarah called it, lead to a verbal fight that escalated to the point where they had not spoken in over a year.

At the time, Sarah cried and said at least her two children had a mother and father who had time for them and weren't focused on just one family member.

Helen too had wept and countered; she had done the best she could.

Old wounds had not healed and were broken open again, wider this time, by harsh words. At the time, Teddy could do little and only wished the hurtful words were not spoken. Many times, illness had taken its toll on the Polinski family and Teddy longed for the quiet, the peace of which television preachers dispensed.

Slowly, Teddy read the letter Sarah sent to mend the fences. He kept it on the coffee table and reread it many times.

Dear Dad,

Please know that I regret losing my temper when you and Mom visited. I truly am sorry for getting angry and yelling at Mom. Recently, I learned from Aunt Edna that Mom is in a nursing home. I hope our argument didn't lead to her getting sick. I feel terribly guilty about all of this.

You know it was hard on me when I was growing-up. Each time you and Mom visited Scott, I stayed at a neighbor's apartment. Many were the nights I ate dinner with their children and barely saw either of you before going to bed. Being shuttled from neighbor to neighbor, I felt like I did not have a family. Other kid's parents helped me with my homework and questioned me about my school activities. It was lonely for me and I felt like I did not belong. Often I cried myself to sleep under the covers so you would not hear.

I promised myself that my children would have two parents who were there for them. I guess, when Mom tried to offer advice about my children, I overreacted. I am sorry, but the hurt has never totally healed.

Please give my love to Mom. Can you forgive me?

Love
Sarah

Slowly, Teddy put down the letter and got up to go to the bathroom. He wondered when he would answer Sarah.

Every day Teddy arrived at the liquor store a few minutes early. He did not like to rush. It was a small store, located in the main shopping center in Coop City. Fred Simon, the store's owner, would be along shortly and then the both of them would open for the day.

Since retiring at age 62 and taking social security, Teddy worked off the books for Fred. The extra money came in handy. Fred and Teddy knew each other before working together for close to ten years. Nightly, after work, Teddy stopped at the store and bought wine for dinner. In time, Fred and Teddy became friends and when Teddy retired from the car dealership in Yonkers, Fred offered Teddy work.

For two years, Teddy worked part-time and enjoyed meeting the different people. Teddy liked helping and being a salesman was as good a way as any. Sales was in his blood and it was easy to switch from cars to 'spirits.' Both were important parts of people's lives.

To get to work, everyone needed a dependable car. Teddy never tried to take advantage or sell someone more than they required. For this, he earned a reputation for honesty. He wanted to see people happy and buying a car could be a happy time. Similarly, liquor helped people to celebrate.

Since Helen became sick, working in the liquor store was more important in helping Teddy to get out of himself. Focusing on the customer pushed Teddy to think about something other than his own problems. The extra money went to purchase little things Scott and Helen required. It felt good to work, meet customers, and contribute to the larger world.

Typically, Sunday was a slow day and the liquor store stayed open until 5 p.m. After work, Teddy walked home from the store and today was no exception. First, he stopped for take-out, vegetable lo mein, and as it was still daylight, walked over to the schoolyard to watch the young basketball players.

Teddy enjoyed watching them play with all their youthful joy and bravado. Even the players, who were not that good, showed off celebrating each basket. As Teddy followed their fast paced three-on-three basketball game, he thought about himself. It had been a very long time since he was happy or enthusiastic about anything. Years of tears and worry burned the enthusiasm away. He could not remember the last time he felt something wonderful would happen in his life.

As Teddy watched the youthful players through the chain link fence that surrounded the schoolyard, he mourned that part of himself. He could not remember when optimism died, but he knew it had. Perhaps his joyful expectation for life was lost on the many trips to the psychiatric hospital. Or it slowly died watching Sarah grow distant, as Helen and he used their energy finding treatment for Scott. If any joy were left, it clearly died the day he admitted Helen to the nursing home.

Slowly, Teddy began to walk toward his apartment. Suddenly, there was the realization of how tired he had become. The Chinese food was still hot, but he no longer was hungry. When he got back to the apartment, he would put the food in the refrigerator for later.

Over the years, so many things had been taken from Teddy. Still, he wondered why he gave up things he enjoyed. He could not control illness or the distance between daughter and parents, but he still could do fun things for himself. It had been years since he went to a baseball game, went fishing, or visited friends. These were parts of life he chose to deny, using Helen as an excuse. If he enjoyed himself, he felt guilty because his loved ones were sick and in pain.

Teddy realized that, if they were asked about the issue, both Scott and Helen would want him to enjoy life. Probably, it would make them feel worse if they knew Teddy gave up things because of them.

As Teddy walked on, he realized thinking about a problem was different than taking action. While he understood that he chose to give up things that made him happy because he felt guilty enjoying himself, restoring the balance and adding enjoyment were harder than thinking about it. Teddy wondered how he could add joy back into his life. Could happiness be added like an ingredient in a recipe? Was it that simple?

Teddy rode the elevator to the 24th floor and mused, more people live in this large building than in the average small town. Thousands of people so close to each other, yet so separate and unaware of what their neighbors think or feel.

Distinct yet connected in some mysterious way. All of these people living in the same building, with similar thoughts and feelings, but not knowing each other's name. Connected by the inner, invisible piece the religious call the human spirit. It was at this level that God supposedly spoke to each person and that everyone was spiritually connected.

Teddy exited the elevator and walked the twenty or so feet to his apartment. All the while, he pondered what God was like. Teddy believed there was a God, and knew God and he were not friends. In Teddy's mind, God never did anything or made an overture that was God-like or special in any way. For Teddy, there had been years of financial struggle and watching those he loved probed by different doctors.

If God were a good father, there were plenty of times God could have extended a helping hand. In Teddy's mind, there had been none of that. Moreover, any future relationship Teddy and God might have had, with Helen now in the nursing home, was shattered. What kind of father does this to his children? Teddy could not reconcile this.

Opening the door to his apartment, Teddy noticed the light flickering on the answering machine. He wondered, who called? Maybe something happened to Scott or Helen? Teddy grew anxious.

Putting down the food on the kitchen table, hesitantly Teddy walked into the living room and played the machine. For an instant, he held his breath, unsure what bad news would be coming his way. "Hello, Dad? Hello, Dad? Are you there?"

It was Sarah's voice and Teddy wondered what terrible news she needed to pass on about her family. Or, not being able to reach him, perhaps the hospital or nursing home somehow got hold of Sarah's phone number? "Well, I guess you're not home. Listen, give me a call. I thought we might get together this week and talk. I really miss you." The message ended.

Still in his zipper jacket, Teddy sat down on the easy chair, relieved nothing bad happened, but nervous about returning Sarah's call. It was a year since they had spoke, when Sarah's hurt feelings resurfaced. Teddy did not want to go through that again. Also, he had not answered Sarah's letter; months had passed since he received it.

It wasn't that Sarah was not entitled to her feelings; clearly, she received the 'short end' growing-up. It was just that Teddy felt it was better to forget about these things. All of that happened a long time ago. Now, it was a time for forgiveness.

Teddy sat in John Wilson's office, waiting for him to return. John was speaking with someone in the reception area. Teddy was passing time, gazing out the window, watching the cars travel the highway. He wondered at the cars speeding up and down the road, people coming and going. To what purpose? People were born, people died. Some were lucky, some were not. Always, Teddy felt he was one of the unlucky ones.

John came back into the office and sat behind his desk. "Sorry to keep you waiting. What's up?"

"We were visiting Scott on the ward, Helen is with him and I thought I'd come by."

"It's always good to see you, Teddy. How are Scott and Helen doing?"

"Both of them are OK."

John paused for a moment, as if he were considering something, and then spoke. "Teddy, have you ever given any thought to why you and I are friends?"

Teddy looked at John and wondered where this came from. He paused and replied, "I thought we liked each other. We met here in the hospital, had something in common, and became friends."

"That is true, but have you ever thought about what we have in common?"

"Well, you work with my son, we are about the same age and just hit-it-off. Beyond that, I haven't given it much thought."

John said, "Well, I have. Now, don't worry, this is not some kind of "come-on," or anything, but I have wondered why you keep coming back. We talk about all kinds of things and do have similar views, but I think you are searching for something."

"What do you mean?" Teddy questioned.

"Well, I know you like getting away from the ward, giving Helen a few minutes alone with Scott. Also, I have such a winning smile and all, but I think you are searching."

"John, I'm having a hard time understanding. Where is this going? I must say, I'm relieved you are not going to ask me out, because I think we would have a difficult time making a go of it... you know, as an interracial couple. It's a hard world out there."

At this remark, John smiled, but continued, "Teddy, I think your spirit is looking for something and knows it can find it here."

As Teddy rested in his easy chair, he wondered why his mind flashed back to that conversation. Right now, he should be calling Sarah on the phone. Instead, his mind jumped to a conversation held years ago, with another person, about what he was searching for.

Although the apartment was air-conditioned and cool, Teddy began to sweat. He stood, took off his zipper-jacket and placed it on the sofa. Boy, his mind was racing all over the place! All this illness had taken its toll. He was beginning to lose it. All these thoughts and ideas, racing through his brain, were troubling. It was not healthy for a person to live alone and under pressure like this. That's why God created man and woman.

"John Wilson, where are you now? Well, if there is a heaven, I know you are up there and hope you are listening. Please put in a good word for me because I am beginning to lose whatever is left of my mind."

At this point, Teddy walked toward the bathroom to shower after a day's work.

The water from the showerhead hit Teddy's body and its pulsating warmth felt relaxing. As the water dripped down his face and caressed his body, Teddy's mind flashed to another time. That magical summer his family went away and he had the season's pass to Paradise Land.

Some days, Teddy spent hours body surfing the waves, merely experiencing the salt-water wash all over him. Riding the waves, feeling their power, Teddy was free. He became the wave. He was outside in the sun and water, racing toward the shore, full of energy. Yes, Teddy was free.

As Teddy lathered the soap and washed himself, he wondered again if he was losing his mind. Admittedly, at this point, there was not much left to lose, but he was beginning to grow concerned. He was thinking far too much about the past, as if he lost something back there and was trying to recapture it.

Sure, he hadn't been happy in a very long time, but in his life there had been few happy people. The people he knew all had their share of misery. The only happy one was now dead. John Wilson, for all his happiness, also endured much pain and died young, at 60, from cancer. Yet, even in his pain, John was joyous. Like Teddy, John spent most of his life around sick people. John had seen affliction up close and personal, but somehow he remained happy.

Stepping out of the shower, Teddy wondered about that.

Riding the train out to Huntington Station, Teddy had a lot of time to reflect and consider how the visit would go. The last visit ended badly, but Teddy had hopes that time would have mended Sarah's wounds and he could enjoy being with his daughter and grandchildren. Sarah's husband, Clay, was at work, leaving Teddy and Sarah to privately discuss what needed to be discussed, hopefully, in a loving, rational manner. Tears. Teddy had seen enough tears and hoped there would be no more.

On Sunday night, it had taken Teddy a couple of hours to find the courage to call his daughter. When he did, the conversation went remarkably well. Sarah invited Teddy for lunch on Tuesday, saying she wanted to mend some fences and get back into his life.

Teddy missed his daughter and wanted to give what, in years past, he had been unable to give. Before it was too late, Teddy wanted to be a part of her life. Circumstances had separated them long enough. Teddy rested his eyes, held Sarah's letter in his hand, while hope fluttered in his heart.

Teddy walked through the train station, which was almost entirely empty this late in the morning. Immediately, he saw Sarah and his granddaughter, Amy, waiting for him. Quickly, Teddy walked toward them, unsure of what to expect. But Sarah opened her arms and gave Teddy a hug and a kiss on his cheek.

The warm welcome put Teddy at ease. He picked-up his granddaughter and carried her as they walked toward the parking lot. Sarah began talking, "Dad, it's good to see you. I've missed you. How are Mom and Scott?"

Teddy replied, "Let's talk about them when we get to your house. For now, let me just look at you and hold Amy. How is Clay? Is Walt at school? I've missed you all very much, you know."

The ride to Sarah's house took fifteen minutes, during which time there was no awkwardness. Teddy felt at ease with his daughter and granddaughter. He caught up on news about Clay and Walt. It was as if no time had elapsed and the year of not speaking had never happened.

After getting Amy settled with lunch and a nap, Teddy and Sarah sat at the kitchen table. They relaxed, drinking coffee and munching on sponge cake. Again, Sarah started the conversation, "Dad, I've missed talking with you. How are Mom and Scott? I'm so upset Mom had to go into a nursing home. It must be lonely for you. I blamed myself. Perhaps, if we didn't argue and yell, she might not have gone into the home. Somehow, I feel responsible."

So there it was, Teddy thought, the terrible guilt that somehow she was the cause of her mother's illness. Teddy paused for a moment, then spoke. "Sarah, don't worry about me. I have plenty to do. I work part-time at the liquor store and visit your Mom and Scott. That keeps me pretty busy. Also, I've learned to shop and do housework.

"You know, you didn't cause your mother to get sick. Yes, she was very upset about the argument and resentment that had built up over the years. But she was grateful that you were able to share the hurt. When she first went into the home, I asked the doctor what had caused her loss of memory and brain function. The doctor said it was something that occurred over time and had been developing for years. He asked me if I noticed early signs of this, moments of confusion, disorientation, memory loss. Afterward, when I thought about it, I guess it had been coming on for a while. The doctor said they knew very little about the cause and scientists were researching medicine to relieve symptoms. He said don't blame yourself."

Sarah replied, "But I do blame myself. I shouldn't have lost my temper and blamed you both for not giving me enough attention. I know you both had your hands full with Scott and I overreacted when Mom tried to offer advice about Amy and Walt. My yelling at her couldn't have helped her condition."

"I know it hurt your mother but I'm sure that argument was not the cause. Perhaps all the years of worrying about you and Scott contributed to the deterioration. But who's to say? The doctors don't know enough and it is easier for me not to search for reasons. This is one of those things about life that's hard to explain.

"Tell me, it must have been hard for you, all those times when you needed our attention, but we were occupied with Scott's problems. You know, I am sorry and regret daily not giving you more. Can you forgive me?"

Sarah stood at the table, bent over and kissed Teddy on the forehead. Slowly a tear trickled down her cheek and she said, "Dad, as I've gotten older, I realize you both did the best you could. I just wish it could have been easier on us all. I love you and Mom. Now, tell me how she and Scott are doing and when I can visit them."

It was late in the evening and Teddy was happy as he rode the train back into the Bronx. The visit had gone very well; better than he could have hoped. He enjoyed being with Sarah and her family.

When they sat outside in the backyard, Teddy had the chance to play catch with both his grandchildren. They tossed around a brightly colored beach ball, laughed and played. At their age, Amy and Walt had so much energy and enthusiasm for life; Teddy had a joyous time.

For a brief moment, it was as if time stood still and Teddy was playing catch with Scott and Sarah. When Teddy tossed the ball to Amy and Walt, it hung suspended in the air and Teddy saw Scott and Sarah in his grandchildren's smiling faces. At that moment, Teddy felt connected to life and it was as if that toss stretched far back into the past and ahead into the future. And Teddy laughed with his children and grandchildren, realizing life could be a smiling, sunny afternoon.

Remarkably, the old feelings of pain, loneliness and struggle were gone. The whole family enjoyed the warm afternoon together. During this time, there was no talk of hospitals and sickness. They simply shared each other's company and laughed.

Looking out the train window and reflecting on the day, Teddy thought of how wonderful life could be. Then, he dozed off.

Dreaming, Teddy found himself back in the state hospital, sitting in John Wilson's office. He and John were in the middle of a conversation and sipping tea.

"Teddy, problems are placed before you so you can overcome them. The illness that beset your family has imposed certain limitations on the way you live and think, yet you must push past or illness will be an impediment in all your lives.

"For example, if you and Helen want to go away on vacation, your first thought will be that you can't go because no one would be here to take Scott the food he likes. Instead, you should be taking a more open view, by thinking that you can go away but need to find someone to bring Scott his treats. Or that Scott will have to make do for two weeks while you are away. You know, either approach is possible.

"Even more insidious is the unconscious relationship that exists between a caregiver and the person they assist. Often, the caregiver binds his or her own happiness to the well being of the person who is ill. Mentally both are linked to the other and the caregiver cannot be happy if the other is unhappy."

Suddenly, Teddy awoke; he was at the last stop. The above ground train had come to a halt and the other passengers were exiting. Teddy got up and followed them down the stairs to the bus stop.

From the train station, it was a ten-minute ride to Coop City and, as Teddy waited for the bus, he struggled to remember his dream. What was his subconscious trying to tell him? Or was John Wilson sending a message from the other side?

"Problems are placed before you so you can overcome them. Be careful tying up your happiness with the happiness of another."

Teddy had not thought about his own happiness in a very long time. Yet, today, with Sarah and her family, he laughed, enjoyed himself and was happy.

Teddy sat and watched the late night news before going to bed. Something was nagging at him, it was just below the surface and he could not get at it. Teddy had lived in his body for a long time and thought he knew where all the potholes were, yet he had apparently stepped into one and it was not one he recognized.

Tomorrow was Wednesday and it was a day to visit Scott and Helen, then go to work. This routine kept him busy, the time went by, but there was no enjoyment or thrill. Over time, these chores lost their excitement and he did them out of obligation rather than enjoyment. Oh, he loved Scott and Helen but sometimes Teddy wanted more. Something he did for himself, something he found exciting.

Surely, he liked being a salesman; meeting people and helping them make decisions. Recently, this too had become tiresome. Gone was the fun. What was nagging at him?

Teddy stood and went into the bathroom to wash up. He turned on the light and examined himself in the mirror. Age had taken its toll. Gone was most of his hair and the few hairs that remained were gray and white. Teddy let the water run in the sink and, when it was hot enough, began splashing it on his face.

Oh, the water felt warm and soothing. It relaxed him. Suddenly, Teddy remembered the dream. Standing outside the fence at Paradise

Stewart Bitkoff, Ed. D.

Land in the dark, wanting to take a last swim and be happy. And the few remaining hairs on Teddy's head stood as he broke into a cold sweat. That dream. What did it mean?

Slowly, Teddy walked back into the living room, turned off the TV and began thinking about the dream and his life. Somehow this dream and the others about John Wilson were connected. His subconscious was trying to send him a message . . . about what was missing in his life? As the night grew darker, Teddy sat in his easy chair and tried to work out the meaning of his dream and his life.

V - Paradise Land

Teddy had not slept all night and, while he had not fully worked out a plan, he knew it was time for action. He enjoyed being with Sarah and her family. This had shown him that life was meant to enjoy, but he had been guilty of "just going through the motions."

Understandably, his attitude was tainted. Always fearing the worst, he merely endured his visits to the state hospital and nursing home. By habit, he went to work, hiding his feelings. He buried and tried to deny them, and was not honest with himself.

Over the years, he lost the joy of life and forgot to be grateful. Sickness beat him down and he had not fought back hard enough to overcome the unhappiness. He let his problems, which were noteworthy, grind him into the dirt. But he could overcome them and still enjoy parts of life. It was a matter of attitude and not confusing one thing with another.

He let life make him a serious 'fuddy-duddy,' forgetting how to be happy and laugh like a young child. Sure, illness and responsibility for family were heavy burdens, at times, but he did not look for joy or happiness in things.

As Teddy dressed, a plan formed. He made himself breakfast and when he finished eating, put his plan into action.

Teddy realized, he was the obstacle in his own path. He was the fence that kept him from Paradise Land. Today, he was going to start climbing that fence.

Teddy had not driven a car in years and was having fun feeling the power and sense of freedom being behind the steering wheel brought. After calling the state hospital, the nursing home, and leaving a message on Fred's answering machine that he would not be coming in, Teddy arranged to rent this car.

Cars had changed since the last time he drove and it took Teddy a few minutes to adjust to all the newer features. He was determined to have fun mastering them all. The satellite navigating system, which provided driving directions from one location to another, only took him a few minutes. He was tired of public transportation and waiting for the bus and the train. While public transportation made sense in the city, so much so that he had sold his car, today something different was taking place. Today he was cutting the old chains and going off in search of a part of himself that he lost.

Teddy realized both the question and answer were inside and he had previously given up on the quest. That was the tragedy. It wasn't so much that life was filled with heartache; it was that he gave up looking for what made him happy. He had resigned himself to unhappiness. The good and bad were both part of the journey. That's what his dreams were trying to tell him.

John Wilson represented that part of himself that was an answer. John was a real person, a good friend who died from cancer, but in Teddy's dreams, John represented more.

As he drove on the highway, Teddy was going against traffic and the satellite navigator helped him not get lost and help him find his way. Most of the traffic was heading into the city and Teddy was going to Far Rockaway. He smiled to himself when he thought about how he handled the clerk at the rental car agency when she asked, "How long will you need the vehicle?" Teddy replied, "I'm not sure."

When she inquired, "How many miles will you put on the car?" He again gave the same answer. However, when she asked, "Is the car for business or pleasure?" Teddy was sure and replied, "Pleasure." In the end, Teddy rented the car for a week, figuring that was enough time to do what he had in mind.

Since he was a teen, Teddy had not been to the beach and Far Rockaway. Part of him was hesitant about intruding upon the past; he realized you could never relive your yesterdays. Consequently, he never took a trip "down memory lane," visiting old neighborhoods or attending reunions. Yet, that was not the point of today's ride. This journey was to set something free and recapture what was lost. He had left something outside the fence at Paradise Land and was going to retrieve it.

As Teddy exited the highway, he could see the roller coaster and different rides. It was late morning; the parking lot was half full and people were beginning to arrive.

After pulling into the parking lot and paying the fee, he parked the car, unsure of what he was going to do next. Teddy was making this up as he went along. He was trying to recapture some of the spontaneity and fun that made life unpredictable and exciting.

Getting out of the car, he could feel the sun growing hot and noticed Paradise Land appeared just like in his dream. From the distance, it looked like the rides and attractions were unchanged. Teddy remembered reading in the paper, or hearing on the news, that the city spent millions restoring the original attractions. This helped create the feeling you were stepping back in time.

Eagerly, Teddy walked toward the main entrance and the swimming pool. The pool was still there, with a chain link fence separating passerby from the crystal clear water. The water appeared as inviting as it did in his dream. Teddy realized why he had come.

For a moment, he stopped outside the fence and gazed at the water. At this early hour, few people were in the pool, the sun was getting hotter and Teddy had packed a swimsuit and towel. Oh, he longed for a swim in the soothing water.

In a matter of minutes, Teddy paid the admission charge and rented a locker. Quickly he entered the locker room, changed, put away his clothes and walked out into the bright sunlight. Finally, he was inside the fence and ready for a swim in Paradise Land.

Teddy walked to the deep end, that part of the pool that faced the street and closest to where he had stood in his dream. This time, unlike his dream, Teddy was inside and ready. He took off his shirt and shoes and then placed his locker key inside his swimsuit pocket before laying his things on a nearby bench. He took a deep breath, closed his eyes and enjoyed the smell of the ocean air as it passed through his nostrils. Walking toward the edge of the pool, he hesitated for a brief moment and leaped. Before hitting the water, Teddy wondered how this experience would change him.

Teddy hit the water and went down, far below the surface, enjoying the cool, refreshing shock. As he held his breath and fell below, he opened his eyes and experienced the soothing, cool water caress his skin. Suddenly, as the water enveloped and cradled his body, he felt recharged and full of energy. Teddy did not want to surface and stayed under water for as long as he could. When he no longer could hold his breath, he swam upward, back toward the sunlight and air. As he broke the water surface, into the sunlight, Teddy yelled out, "Hooray!" He was renewed, grateful to be alive.

Teddy floated, caught his breath and rested. Then, he gazed at the street, through the chain link fence, and smiled. Next, he began swimming across the water. As he swam, Teddy thought it felt good to swim and exercise. It was relaxing. Next, he decided to do laps and started swimming back and forth, using a slow, methodical breaststroke.

As Teddy felt the warm sun on his head and the cool water against his body, he realized he had been wrong. He could be happy. All he needed was the courage to change. He needed to be the one to climb the fence and break down the barriers that stood between him and happiness. As the morning sun grew hotter, Teddy frolicked in the cool water of Paradise Land.

Feeling refreshed and relaxed, Teddy bought himself a large soft pretzel and bottle of Yoo-Hoo chocolate drink. He sat in the shade to dry and mused, "This snack brings back memories, a time when I was young and optimistic about life. Over the years, as different problems arose, somehow I lost the zest for trying new things. Sadly, the only adventures I had were painful, but life is both misery and joy. I became lazy and did not pursue enjoyment.

"I like the smell of the ocean, watching the gulls glide on the wind, and the bathers riding the waves. This was here all the time and I neglected to make time for myself."

Renewed, driving back to the Bronx, Teddy was planning the route to complete the next part of the journey. An "old bill" was past due and again, he had waited too long to do what was right.

Driving along at 55 mph, feeling the air conditioner against his skin, Teddy felt alive. He approached the Whitestone Bridge, dug into his pocket to find the correct change for the toll and could feel the anxiety in his stomach mount. In some ways, the things he was doing, after putting them off for years, helped reconnect him with the world. The sadness was gone and Teddy felt brand new.

After paying the toll, Teddy remembered the Westchester Square Exit would be coming up quickly on the right. From there, he would take a right and follow Tremont Avenue until he saw the entrance and office. At this time of the afternoon, traffic was light and Teddy reached where he was going in ten minutes.

As he pulled into the cemetery, surprisingly, Teddy found himself saying a silent prayer. He was asking God for strength and wondered, to himself, why he was doing this. Looking around seeing the hundreds who passed over made Teddy anxious and instinctively a part of him knew, on this sacred ground, the direction to turn. Few people were visiting this Wednesday afternoon and it was getting very hot.

Teddy stopped his car, went into the cemetery office and made an inquiry about plot location. Fortunately, it was cool in the office and, as soon as Teddy got back into the car, he turned the air conditioning up. The short walk out in the sun, from the office to the car, made the sweat pour down his face. Suddenly, with the growing heat and anxiety in his stomach, Teddy felt very uncomfortable. Should a Jew visit a Christian cemetery? He wondered if he were doing the right thing. Of course he was, he told himself, and drove slowly to the sector set aside for clergy and their family.

It took a few minutes to find the plot. The satellite navigator wasn't up for this task and Teddy relied on his sense of direction. Once Teddy found the plot, he sat in the car and tried to collect his thoughts. He wondered why he had not gone to the funeral or paid his respects earlier. Teddy really did not have a good excuse; he had not gone because he said funerals made him feel uncomfortable and if there was life after death, his friend could hear him no matter where he was.

Teddy understood, as he got out of the car and walked toward the headstone that respect had to be shown to the deceased reaching outside of oneself and giving back. That was what the journey to the grave, in part, meant; you did something for someone else. In addition, there was the family of the deceased and, by attending the funeral, you were in some way connecting with and easing their grief.

Teddy stood in front of John Wilson's grave, feeling the hot summer sun on his back. Here was an opportunity for Teddy to do the right thing and pay an "old bill."

Hesitating for a moment, considering what to say, he then recalled advice an old friend gave, "Just say what is in your heart."

Teddy let the words flow. "John, old friend, I have thought of you often. Rarely was the day that I did not recall a conversation and some advice you gave. Oh, I miss our talks, and lately you have been popping up in my dreams. I guess there is something I over-looked or did not get quite right.

"Forgive me for not coming to the funeral but I was weak and ducked my responsibility. Avoiding responsibility seems to be something I have done often. Oh, I visited the sick, Scott and Helen, regularly went to work, but I have been avoiding the responsibility of making something more of my life. I stumbled and did not pick myself up. Because I felt guilty, I sacrificed those things that made me happy and became a bitter old man.

"God dealt me a difficult hand and, over the years, I became angry. I lost my sense of gratitude for everything else that was given. I let the anger at God hold down the love and joy that was in my heart.

"When you became sick with the cancer, still you came to work and were filled with joy and excitement. When I questioned how you continued to work for God after you were stricken with cancer, you replied that you were filled with tears and anger, but life was more than tears and anger. You said the balance must be maintained; we were also created to love, work, laugh and serve.

"At the time, I thought you were repeating platitudes to help yourself believe them. Helen's sickness caused me to go deeper and look for meaning. At first, it was easy to be beaten down by a new problem, another illness visited upon our family. Certainly, as a result of Scott's mental illness, we did our share of wondering and crying.

"When Helen was placed in the home, the old doubts and questions came back. This hurt was very deep, but in the hurt I traveled to another part of myself. Slowly, I realized my life was more than it appeared. Beyond the pain and eventual death, were joy, peace and happiness.

"First, I had to take positive action and reach out. For when we reach out to God, God reaches out to us. These last two days, visiting my grandchildren and daughter, and fulfilling one of my dreams with God's Mercy, hope has rekindled in my heart. I did something for someone else. I went to see my daughter and helped ease her pain and guilt about her mother's illness. Also, I played with my two grandchildren and took a swim in the water of Paradise Land. These things filled me with joy and I realized anew we are responsible for our own life and enjoyment.

"John, when I came to visit you in your office, I know you told me this many ways and times. Well, it took awhile... but the advice finally took.

"I regret that I did not come to your funeral and offer condolences to your wife and daughters. This is something I am still ashamed about but realize that, if you were alive you would say, 'remember, there is no time and distance for love.' Love is like the summer sun, it fills the air with light and gives life to everyone, no matter how distant they may be from the source."

Teddy walked from his friend's grave, got into the rental car and felt at peace. He sat quietly for a few moments, looking at the gravestone, and realized that one day, he too would be in the ground. Now, while he was alive, he was given the opportunity to make something out of his life. As God wills, Teddy resolved to do positive things with the remaining time he had.

Teddy realized he had been angry and did his best to deny and fight against God. In denying God, Teddy knew he denied a part of himself. In time, he hoped God would forgive him.

That evening, as Teddy sat in his easy chair at the apartment in Coop City, he felt at peace and happy. The over riding anxiety and sadness that had been his companion for so many years now, was replaced with hope and optimism.

Teddy knew joy and happiness, like everything in life, were temporary and it was his responsibility to make life meaningful. He had to be the one to fill his life with positive activities and friends. He had to reach for things that were important and gave him pleasure.

As he rested, Teddy made a list of things that made him happy and resolved to do at least one of these daily. This was his happiness calendar.

VI – Happiness

Teddy realized he made a mistake in thinking. He believed happiness was dependent upon events. This is partially true, as sometimes happiness is connected to events, but there is another kind of happiness. This more independent, more lasting happiness is a spiritual state of being.

In the past, when good things happened Teddy was happy. When he got a raise at work, or a new car, life was good. Similarly, life was bad when they got a call from the hospital when Scott was in a fight or when Teddy did not have enough money to pay a bill.

Very late in life, Teddy learned the trick was to be happy in spite of bad things happening. To be dependent upon external events and others for joy was a fool's game. Teddy found something deeper, in the very depth of his soul.

Joy and happiness were an inner spiritual condition, a peace and harmony where you were grateful for being alive and took pleasure in life. Happiness meant being involved with others and connected to God, drawing strength from the reservoir of your own soul. There was a part of you that was independent of life and when your body died this part continued. The soul was always with God and, to realize this, all you need do was dive into the water of your soul.

This spiritual strength and wisdom were the water Teddy climbed the fence to experience. The fence was his expectation, or mindset, and happiness was dependent upon others and events. This water, of God's Love and Mercy, was deep inside of Teddy. Swimming in the cool, clear water of Paradise Land helped Teddy remember this essential truth. Everything you need for the journey is already inside you.

As Teddy prepared for his morning of visiting Scott and Helen, he realized life had ups and downs but, far below the surface; there was always the still water of Paradise Land. To take a swim and restore balance and happiness, all he had to do was turn inward.

Life was filled with misery. Similarly, life was filled with joy and fun things to do. That was what John Wilson tried to teach Teddy;

while John struggled with cancer and painful chemical treatments, John urged Teddy to drink of his own spirit.

John once claimed, "Happiness is found by turning inward, by thanking God for all God gives. It is found in helping others, as God's servant; by being part of life and grateful for the beauty around you. This change in thinking, or awareness, was only possible through a spiritual awakening." Teddy found his awakening in the cool, crystal water of Paradise Land.

Now that Teddy realized this, how was he going to put this wisdom into practice? That was the challenge of each day and as Teddy got ready to leave his apartment, he spoke to God and requested God's help. Teddy walked through the door of his apartment, realizing God was always present. He had forgotten this and missed the point of sickness. Suffering could be transcended and, while Paradise Land was located in Far Rockaway, it was also a place deep within. Teddy had a season pass. All he had to do to jump the fence of his negative thoughts and turn toward God.

We were born to be happy. We forget this. Sadly, we look to the world and events for completeness, instead of swimming in our own spiritual water.

As Teddy rode the elevator down from the 24th floor, he was confident his life was changing, and with God's help, Teddy would be happy each day.

Teddy pulled the rental out of the garage, adjacent to his building. After he paid the overnight parking fee, Teddy decided to buy a car. In the city, there were additional expenses but, at this point in life, he needed the freedom car ownership provided.

Perhaps he would take a vacation, drive out to Colorado and see his sister, June. She lived in the mountains outside of Denver and he had never been there; there were so many places he wanted to visit.

Waiting for the traffic light to change, Teddy began making a mental list of things he needed to do:

- Teddy realized that happiness was transitory and would come and go. Depending upon many factors, it was not a static mental state.

- Often it was the small things in life that people enjoyed most: visiting the grandchildren, going for a swim, or driving a car. Teddy was going to add these things daily to his list.

- Teddy needed to be with people and share his life with them. In addition, he needed some alone time to turn inward and needed to plan these times so that the correct spiritual balance was maintained.

- He needed to be part of the world and help others. While he was able to do this as part of his sales job, Teddy wondered if he should develop other ways.

The traffic light changed and the cars behind were honking their horns, telling Teddy to get moving. Teddy turned on his directional and made a left onto the highway entrance ramp. He accelerated and merged into the highway traffic, wondering if it were possible to be happy in the middle of all the torment of the state hospital?

When he asked John Wilson this question, John replied, "Lasting peace and happiness is only found in love of God. Certainly, as I seek to help those who are troubled, I am affected deeply by their pain but it is possible to have two things in your heart. Compassion is born of inner peace and love.

"Why God created a world where pain is as common as laughter, that, my friend, is something you must experience and it is a spiritual state."

As Teddy continued driving south and saw the tan brick buildings of the state hospital, he knew his newly found peace and contentment was about to be tested. When he saw Scott, Teddy wondered, would he remain happy?

Also, Teddy realized that no matter what happened in the hospital to upset him or Scott, joy was within reach. The refreshing water of Paradise Land was always available and Teddy could go for a swim any time he wanted. All he had to do was say a prayer. Paradise Land was within and fed by the water of God's Love and Mercy.

VII – Moving On

The silence was broken and the Master continued. "There are two kinds of happiness. The first is the happiness that is tied to the world and events. Depending upon circumstance, it comes and goes and is the more fragile. The second is spiritual contentment, which is accompanied by a silent, loving peace. This is the more lasting and is found in your soul.

"Like the waves on top of the ocean, life's events are a series of ups and downs. Yet, far below the surface, the water is peaceful and still. This peace and joy is found by swimming in the deep, quiet water of your soul.

"And as the student becomes more adept, he can enter this state, simply by turning inward."

Over the following months, as Teddy's life became filled with different interests and began to change, I saw less and less of him. One time we met on a sunny afternoon in City Island and went sailing. Teddy was taking lessons and took me along. We had a grand time laughing and making all kinds of mistakes together.

Another time Teddy invited me to go with him and a young man to a New York Yankee baseball game. Teddy had become a 'Big Brother' and was mentoring this teenager. All three of us enjoyed the game, discussing strategy and watching the different people in the crowd.

One other special time, we met at the Metropolitan Museum of Art. Teddy took up oil painting and wanted some inspiration from the masters. On this occasion, we had plenty of time to talk and I caught up on news about Teddy's family.

Sadly, there had been little change in Helen and Scott's health and Teddy continued to visit on a weekly basis. Also, Teddy had become a regular part of Sarah's life and helped 'baby-sit' his grandchildren, attending their various activities.

When I questioned Teddy about these changes and the enthusiastic way he quickly added so many experiences, he replied,

"These things were already inside, waiting to come out. I just learned to trust and follow my own inner wisdom."

As I sat and listened to Teddy happily talking about different topics and new interests, I blurted out, "Teddy, how did you learn to trust your own inner wisdom?"

Teddy paused and smiled. He hesitated, as if he were considering what to say. Then offered, "Young fella, I guess you have not been listening closely all of these months to my story, have you?"

As time passed, I've had time to consider what I learned. The following excerpt from one of Teddy's letters says it all. Incidentally, he did take that trip to Colorado and visit his sister June.

"You know, no one is promised tomorrow. All we have is this day and moment. If there is something you want to do, and it will make you or someone you love happy, do it. Do it now. Do not rely on someone else for your happiness. Just as you are responsible for helping your family, working and contributing to the world, you are responsible for your own spiritual peace and contentment.

"Do not blame others if you are unhappy. Work for what brings you pleasure. Remember: turn inward. You have a season pass and the hour grows late."

Book 3

The Judgment of Julie

The Song Bird

The student questioned, "Master, please help me. I have pondered the riddle and my mind aches from trying to work out the answer."

The Master replied, "Little one, the mind was not created to work out this problem; the answer comes from the heart. The mind's job is to ask. Since you have worked, struggled, and now requested assistance, I will provide the answer."

It matters not to the songbird
If other birds are there to hear its song.
The song and sweet melody
Arise from the heart and the notes must be sung.
The mountains, lakes, flowers and streams
Sway to the bird's song;
They listen with an inner ear.

It is the same
With a man's life.
Each has a song to sing
And it matters not

126

If others are there
And hear the tune.
For it is the song of creation;
This song must be sung
And in the singing is the joy.

****

I – Introduction

How do you measure the worth of a person's life? What criteria do you use to evaluate the total of seventy years? In tallying, is success in the market-place as important as being a loving parent and grandparent? In part, these questions and their answers are the subject of this tale. Julie's journey and struggle to evaluate the significant events and learning experiences of his life, hopefully, will help you further develop your own answer to these important questions.

Before we begin, let me give you some background information about the characters. For purposes of confidentiality, names and individual events have been changed.

In the year 1907, Julius (Julie) Simkus at the age of 19 came through Ellis Island. Like millions of other immigrants before and after, Julius left his home, a small village in eastern Russia, to come to America to make a better life.

Julius married Reba Bernstein, had three children and eight grandchildren. Julie never made much money and at times was not a very good husband. Yet, most of the time he was a loving and compassionate father and grandfather. Julie and Reba raised their children in Brooklyn, New York.

In 1965, Julie died at the age of 76 from colon cancer, an illness he was slow to get treated. Reba lived another four years and did not remarry. At the age of 80, she died (1969) in their small apartment in a New York City public housing development.

Julie, an Orthodox Jew, was the son of an honored Rabbi and philanthropist, rebelled against this heritage. As a young man, Julie liked "wine, women, and song" and was a painful scandal to his father. Fleeing from the small village in Russia to avoid conscription into the Czar's Army, Julie came to America without a trade or a way to make a living.

Financially, in America Julie struggled and often it was up to Reba to keep the family together. Living rent free as superintendents who cared for a large apartment building, Reba was the one who took out the garbage cans and did the building chores. As a tailor, Julie was lucky to find work 2 months a year and, seemingly physically healthy, was never able to work long periods to support his family.

Still, with all these limitations, to me, Julie was someone special. I still remember the love he gave us each Sunday when we visited. And as he got older, I still have a memory of Julie praying, in prayer shawl and yarmulke, each afternoon before we arrived, standing by the window in their bedroom. Most of all, I cherish a special act of kindness.

Yes, there were things about Julie that were scandalous but there were also things about him that were loving and wonderful. According to our religion, on the Judgment Day, like everyone else, Julie will stand before God and ask to account for the good and evil that he did. According to the ledger count, then God will decide Julie's judgment.

Today, by our material standards, most would say Julie fell short of the mark and his potential.

In this story, the tallying-up of things is done a little differently.

II - Simkus Family Tree

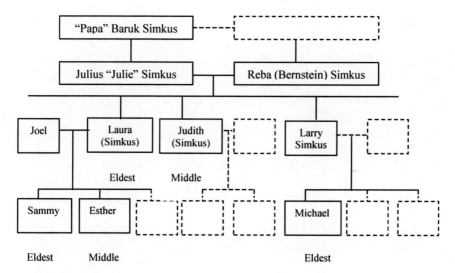

* Family members are not listed unless they are mentioned (by name) in the story.

*Julie and Reba had three children (Laura, Judith, Larry); all three married and had eight grand children.

III - The Apartment on Union Avenue

Slowly, Julie opened his eyes and began to sit-up in bed. Surprisingly, he was no longer in pain and most of the restlessness was gone. The afternoon nap, brief as it was, helped Julie forget about his problems. He was now rested and less anxious.

Sitting on the edge of the bed, looking around the bedroom he and Reba had shared for nearly 20 years, Julie felt there was something different. Taking an inventory, Julie observed that the pictures of Papa Baruk and Sammy were on the wall. The chest of drawers, where he and Reba kept their clothes, was beside the bed. The wooden closet was in the corner. All these things were in place, yet, something just didn't seem right.

Growing more restless, Julie stood and walked into the living room. He called, "Reba, Reba, are you there?" As Julie walked from the living room into the kitchen and the bathroom, there was no sign of Reba. The apartment was empty. Julie wondered, perhaps she was out front sitting and talking? Julie wasn't much for conversation. Often, Reba went outside to talk with the other women.

Next, Julie got a pot from inside the stove, filled it with water, turned on the burner, and waited for the water to boil. After a nap, he liked hot tea and enjoyed smelling the vapors as they rose from the steaming cup. Waiting for the water to boil, Julie realized his stomach no longer ached and burned. The intense pain that he had felt, on the left side of his stomach shooting through to his rear, was gone. Yes, it had been a good nap. Once again, sleep had somehow gotten rid of the terrible pain. This was temporary; always the pain returned.

Reba kept telling him to go to the doctor but Julie refused. Once those doctors got their hands on you, nothing good ever happened. They took your money, gave you pills, and still you suffered. By not going, at least he didn't owe money that he didn't have. After paying rent and buying food, there was no extra money for doctors. So his stomach hurt; he was used to the pain.

Hearing the water boil, Julie got up and poured some hot water onto the tea bag in his cup. Waiting for the tea to steep, Julie carried the tea into the living room. He placed the cup on the small table beside his favorite chair and began to sit down. Surprisingly, Julie felt no pain as he bent and sat back into his easy chair. As he inhaled the sweet smell of the tea, Julie wondered how long Reba would be gone. He wanted to tell Reba that he was feeling better and apologize for yelling at her when she insisted that he go to the doctor.

Julie reached into his vest pocket for his watch to check the time. He had been in so much pain that he had gone to bed with his clothes on. Searching his vest and trouser pockets, he couldn't find his watch. Usually, he had his watch with him at all times; it was his most precious possession. The gold pocket watch was the first thing Julie had bought for himself in America.

Over 50 years ago, after he had gotten his first job in the garment district, Julie saved for months to buy the watch. After paying his board in the rooming house, there had not been much left over. It took 6 long months but he saved the money. Then, Julie went to the pawnshops on Broadway and, after hours of searching and haggling on price, found the perfect gold watch and chain. The pawnshop owner said it had been made in Switzerland and would keep time for another 100 years.

Julie laughed to himself as he recalled the conversation; he wouldn't need the watch to last that long. Seventy-five years would be plenty of time. In his family, unless they went to war, men lived into their 80's and 90s.

As Julie sipped his tea, he wondered what was keeping Reba. He wanted to apologize for getting angry. Maybe this was the thing that was making him feel uneasy. He shouldn't have yelled. Over the years, his temper and stubbornness had gotten him into all kinds of problems.

As Reba looked out the window, she wondered where all the time had gone. Just like this speeding car, the hours of their life together had raced by.

Reba fought back the tears and was grateful that his suffering had past. Her poor Julie, the pain in his stomach now gripped her heart.

Julie was growing more restless and began to pace about the apartment. He walked into the bedroom, then back into the kitchen before sitting down in the living room. Preoccupied, he couldn't sit still, pondering the whereabouts of his watch.

Again, he got up to look through his clothes in the chest of drawers and closet. He searched the bed, even under the mattress. Where had he put it?

Perhaps Reba took it to the jeweler for cleaning? No, Reba wouldn't do that without telling him first. She knew better than to touch his things. And where was Reba? She should have been back by now; it was time to get supper started.

As Julie paced and searched for his lost pocket watch, the anxiety continued to build. What was bothering him? Something was not right; he could feel it in his stomach. This time, Julie had to make sure that he didn't take out the burning in his gut on Reba when she returned.

Oh, the terrible pain in his stomach was now replaced with a churning anxiety.

Judith, the second oldest daughter, was seated beside Reba and held Reba's hand as she stared out the car window. Their car was following the hearse as it made its way across the Verrazano Bridge to the cemetery in Staten Island.

"Mama," Judith said, "Are you alright? You have not said a word since we left the Funeral Home in Brooklyn. You know, it's good to talk about it."

Slowly, Reba turned toward Judith and smiled through her tears. Reba whispered, "I will miss him so much."

Judith put her arms around Reba and hugged her. Judith replied, "I will miss him too."

Julie decided to call out the window for Reba. He was tired of wondering about his watch and was getting hungry for supper. Julie wanted to know what she was cooking, though he knew that Reba didn't like it when he called for her. She thought it embarrassing and told him never to do it, but Julie wanted his watch and was hungry.

Decidedly, he got up from his easy chair, walked into the kitchen and pulled the cord on the window shade. The shade jumped up and as Julie reached to raise the window, he was puzzled. There was no street. As Julie looked through the glass for the other buildings, he started to get nervous. They were all gone and there was no pavement, people, or cars below the window. Somehow, Julie forced himself to raise the window to get a better view. As he looked further, he saw none of the familiar landmarks, only a soft-white, pulsating cloud of light.

To make sure, he raised the window higher and stuck his head completely outside. He looked below where Reba usually sat and chatted with her friends, his heart beginning to race; there was no front of the building. It was gone. Only soft-white, pulsating clouds of light were to be seen.

Where was Reba? Where was he? Julie didn't know what to do. Perhaps his mind was playing tricks on him? Over the last few weeks, he had been in a great deal of pain. Quickly, Julie pulled himself together and walked into the living room. He raised the shades on each of the two windows. It was the same. There was nothing but the soft, glowing light outside. There was no fire escape or other buildings and no street below.

By this time, Julie was sweating and walked into the bedroom. Pulling aside the curtains on the window, he looked outside. It was the same; nothing but the white, pulsating light.

Julie sat on the bed and began to wonder, what had become of him? Was he dreaming? Was he going crazy? Then, Julie's stomach began to ache; it was that familiar, burning pain that shot from the left middle of the stomach all the way into his rear.

The pain became severe and he had to lie down, holding his stomach and calling out, "Oh, Lord, what have you done to me?" As Julie continued to pray, he was able to slowly force some of the pain from his mind and go back to sleep. It was not a deep sleep, but that middle place between being awake and asleep. Somehow he had to escape the pain and the soft-white, pulsating light outside.

"Brrinng." "Brrinng." "Brrinng." Julie awoke to the ringing of the apartment doorbell. Slowly, he got out of bed and put on his slippers. Walking from the bedroom, through the living room and into the kitchen, as he neared the front door, the ringing continued. Julie called out, "Alright already. I'm coming."

Nervously, Julie approached the door. Not sure what he would find on the other side, he paused for a moment and remembered looking outside the windows. There was nothing; only the soft white light. Julie wondered, what kind of dream seemed so real? Was it the stomach pain finally pushing the mind over the edge?

Julie froze and decided he would not open the door. If this were a dream, he would simply wait and see what happened next. "Brrinng." The doorbell continued to ring.

Julie was frightened. He stood in the kitchen, about four feet from the door and thought that maybe, if he stood real quiet, whoever was ringing the bell would go away. He could wait. If it was Reba, she had a key. If she left her key in the apartment, she could get their neighbor, who kept a spare key for them, to unlock the door. Sure, Reba would be angry that he hadn't opened the door, but Julie was frozen with fear. He didn't know what to do, thinking to himself, I am losing my mind. I cannot even decide to open the door.

Then, Julie heard someone call his name. "Julius, open the door, I know you are there. Open the door."

No one had called him Julius in years. The voice was familiar and, without thinking, Julie moved to the door, undid the two locks and opened it.

When he saw who was standing in the hall, Julie nearly fainted. His knees grew weak and he grasped for breath. Stammering, Julie said, "Papa Baruk . . . What are you doing here? You can't be alive. I saw you last nearly 60 years ago when I ran away to America. Now, you must be over 100 years old. Yet, you look the same as the day I left. How can that be?"

Papa Baruk looked lovingly at Julie and softly said, "Son, may I come in?"

Julie replied slowly, "Yes."

Julie was busy preparing tea for his father. He was standing beside the stove, lighting one of the burners. His hand was shaking and he was afraid to speak. His mind raced, how could Baruk be here? How did he find me? I ran away from Russia so many years ago and never contacted anyone.

Baruk had taken off his long coat and placed it on one of the kitchen chairs. He was standing and waiting for Julie to sit. Baruk did not know which chair to take; he was the guest and waited.

Noticing that his father was standing, Julie turned and said, "Father, please have a seat." Julie sat at the head of the table, in the chair closest to the stove. Baruk sat in the chair next to Julie that faced the kitchen wall and spoke.

"Julius, my son, how are you feeling?"

Julie hesitated, afraid to speak, thinking for a long, endless moment about what to say. With Baruk, Julie never got anything right. He was the black sheep of the family, the drunken womanizer. Baruk was the great man; the landowner, the wise Rabbi, the philanthropist who suffered the shame of Julie's youthful excess.

In part, that was why Julie fled, never again to see his family. He ran away because of the embarrassment he had become. Also, he ran from conscription in the Czar's army. Julie knew he was not disciplined enough to become part of that life and realized he would die in battle or desert. So, like a thief in the night, he ran to America.

Now it was time to pay the bills. Surely Baruk was here to collect and make Julie pay emotionally. Julie could never stand beside Baruk and do the things Baruk had done. In America, as a tailor, Julie never got enough work to make ends meet; often Reba had to find part-time jobs. The work of a tailor was below Julie's station; as a Kohen, a descendent from the line of Aaronic Priests, Julie was expected, minimally, to enter one of the professions. Back home, he had refused every training opportunity and never took school seriously. He was too busy with drink and tavern girls.

Well, now the bills were due and Julie was ready. He had rehearsed this meeting, in his mind, many times. There was much to talk about and, although fearful, Julie welcomed the opportunity to say what had to be said.

Julie looked at Baruk who was waiting patiently for Julie to speak. Baruk appeared exactly as memory served; black beard and long black hair with a hint of gray, atop his head the Rabbi's Yarmulke, dark vest and pants with a white shirt. Even in the hottest weather these garments were worn. Julie never understood how this clothing helped his father feel closer to God.

In fact, as a young man, Julie resented Baruk's relationship with God. Julie resented the hours that Baruk prayed and listened patiently to other people's problems. Baruk never took the time to listen to

Julie's problems. Later, when it was too late, Julie realized that Baruk had tried to comfort and guide but Julie had never let Baruk in.

Each time Baruk had knocked on the door, Julie locked it. So many opportunities to love and have comfort missed.

Julie inquired, "Father, do you still like your tea sweet with honey?"

Baruk replied, "Yes, Julius. The tea is welcome but that is not why I have come."

"Why have you come?"

"To help you."

"Why? Do I need your help?" asked Julie.

Baruk paused, looked deeply into his son's eyes and whispered, "Julius, where are you? Do you really think you are still on Union Avenue?"

With these words, Julie began to feel the knot in his stomach grow tighter. Julie paused, thought hard, and finally knew where he was.

Slowly Julie questioned, "I am in the next place and have passed over?"

"Exactly Julius," whispered Baruk.

At this confirmation, Julie mumbled, "Then, what of Reba and the others?"

"Do not worry about them. Julius, One who loves them more than you or I is looking after their needs. Now you must use this time for yourself. It is what you need and wanted. This is your place, Julius, your time. When this time is over, then you will move on. I am here to help you. It is what you wanted."

Shiva was being held in Esther's house. Laura, the eldest of Reba and Julie's three children, shared a mother and daughter with Esther. After the funeral, as was the custom, the family got together to comfort each other.

Reba was numb from the long ride between Staten and Long Island. Reba thought to herself, it was good to have Judith guide her through the difficult portions of the day. Now the question of which one of them would go first was answered. It was so like Julie to take the easy way and leave her behind, so she would miss him.

Julie had taken the next step and now was on the other side. According to tradition, a family member would be there to greet Julie; Reba wondered if this was true. It was comforting to believe that a family member would be there to help Julie adjust. She hoped that he would find peace and comfort on the other side. He suffered so, not wanting to go to the doctors and afraid of what they would find.

Julie had thought he could pray away the pain and sickness. Perhaps this was true sometimes, but not this time. Not this time . . . Oh, Julie, why were you so stubborn? Perhaps, if you had listened and gone to the doctors sooner, both you and I would be visiting Esther's house to see our grandchildren, not to mourn your passing.

"Papa, this is not the way I pictured heaven. It is heaven, isn't it? I'm not in the other place, am I?" Receiving no answer, Julie slowly continued. "Papa, as I got older, I tried to live a better life. Really, I tried to be a good person. I prayed in the morning and evening. I gave to the Shul and helped care for the unfortunate. We were a poor congregation. I did the best I could. Papa, please answer, where am I?"

"Julius, this is the place you go immediately after the physical death. It is not heaven or hell. Heaven and hell is an idea that has been placed in your mind and the way you expect the after-life is not the way it is. This picture of heaven and hell is based upon fear and reward. The reality is other than this."

"Then, where am I?"

"Julius, for the most part, you are in your own mind. This place, the people who visit and some of the experiences are all thoughts. They are extensions of your mind and are connected to the Light so you can unravel the meaning of your life. This is the time and place you are given to choose your own direction. After death, each soul looks at its own life and evaluates the actions. This, the soul does on its own with guidance. After this period, it moves on to the next place to learn, work and serve."

"Papa, what are you saying? This place, this apartment, your visit are creations of my mind. How can that be? Where are the clouds? The Angels? The Devil? Were these things made up?"

"Julius, if you wish to see Angels or Devils, that is up to you. Here in this place, in this time, you can create whatever you wish. It is a time to evaluate the measure of your life. You have as much time as you need. For this portion, your higher soul will guide. That part is always in tune with the higher destiny of the universe and the Light."

"Papa, then you are not real. You are not actually here?"

"Julius, I am here. You called me here to assist in your transition. As it was in keeping with your need and the destiny of the universe, I am here to help you. In time, you will better understand how this place, and the next, works."

With Baruk's words, Julie closed his eyes and couldn't say anything more. He didn't know what to say; he just sat at the kitchen table in his old apartment in Brooklyn, silently repeating the prayer for the dead.

Reba needed a few minutes of peace and quite and hid from the others in the bathroom. She needed the time to be alone and think. The last two days had been a whirlwind. Unconscious, Julie was rushed to the hospital in an ambulance and never awoke. Reba had been unable to rouse him from an afternoon nap.

From that point on, it was one thing after another; notifying the children, Laura, Judith and Larry; making arrangements for the burial; calling Julie's friends at the Shul. Reba had barely enough time to catch her breath.

Reba never understood, in their religion, why the rush to put the loved one in the ground. Certainly, in older times it made sense; the body rotted and everyone was prone to disease. The damn flies alone were enough to test your patience . . .

Certainly, the Goyum were a little bit more civilized about everything. They waked the body for days, filling it with liquids to preserve the flesh. This gave the family time to adjust to the idea that their loved one was gone.

Oh God, she was going to miss Julie. Who was she going to cook for and argue with? The children were all grown with their own families. Now, it was just her. Oh Julie, why had you been so stubborn about going to doctors?

Suddenly, Julie found himself being lifted and transported out of his apartment, through the Light, and into a place that was filled with loving, peaceful energy, wisdom and creative potential. While Julie did not visually recognize anything in this place, his soul knew the different beings who appeared as clusters of light and recognized the energy. The beings of light varied in intensity from a very low, white hue to a brightly burning, blue-white light.

Present in the circle of these beings were a dozen of these clusters. Without a word being spoken, space was made for Julie to join. And, as these beings pulsated with loving energy, Julie felt communication being passed between them. No words were spoken, yet Julie understood a sharing of wisdom and creative potential was occurring.

Julie gazed around at the others and then looked more closely at himself. He was the same as they but a little different; still there remained an outline of his physical body. While his intensity of light was low, it was aglow with a burning, peaceful energy. Instantly, Julie recognized this as his primal-self; the soul, the center of his being.

As Julie sat in the circle with the other clusters of light, he felt at peace. Passing the energy between them, answering questions without the words being spoken, this energy was their home. It was always present and Julie was kept alive by this energy.

Here Julie stayed for a period that had no beginning or end. It always was and, as Julie drank of this energy, he recognized the Source and knew that part of him was always at peace, always at one with the Life Force.

When Julie opened his eyes, he again found himself sitting at the kitchen table. Baruk was still there and smiling at his son. Sensing Julius's momentary confusion, Baruk waited patiently.

After a time, Baruk began, "So Julius, we have some business to catch up with. That is why I am here. What is it that you want to say?"

Julie paused, summoning up his courage and trying to recall what he wished to say. For a long time, Julie wanted to ease the pain he had caused his father.

"Papa, you were right. I wasted what I was given and all my life I struggled because of it. I am sorry for the hurt I caused you. I should have applied myself and learned a trade so that when the time came I could better care for my family.

"I wish that I had never run away and turned my back on you. Can you forgive me?"

"Oh Julius, you were the sunshine of my day and, after your mother died, you were the main source of joy in my life. I always loved you and never wanted any harm to come to you. Early on, I saw that you were your own worst enemy and had to dance across the flame. Nightly I prayed that you would not hate me and have an easier way. Yet, your destiny was to learn by climbing the steep path and falling into the fire.

"The fact that you ran away to America saved your life; you never could have lasted in the Army and would have landed in prison or been shot as a deserter. You were not cut from that cloth. I only wish you had written to me."

For a timeless moment both father and son gazed into each other's eyes and their souls joined, rejoicing in reconciliation and love. Here the two stayed, entwined in each other's light until the old wounds were healed and each was set free by love and forgiveness.

Reba walked among family and guests. She was trying to be sociable and thanked each for coming and supporting her during this difficult time. The adults were talking and eating and the children were running about playing tag. This made Reba happy and she thought to herself, life went on. One life passed into the other world and, in time, another would enter this one. These things had their own rhythm and it was difficult to guess the meaning of it all.

The young ones running about gave little thought to death and the purpose of life. This subject was for the old people; the Rabbis and philosophers who were closer to it. This was the way it was and should be. Or should it?

Reba wondered, shouldn't each person, as early as possible, come to some understanding about these things? That is what the great religions taught. Wasn't each soul a traveler through the many worlds on their way back to God? Certainly Orthodox Jews viewed the travel of men and women differently. One was the weaker vessel and, by nature, did not have the capacity to examine or discuss these great mysteries. Reba disagreed.

When Reba tried to engage Julie in discussion about the afterlife, he wasn't willing. Julie said, "About these things, let women speak with women and men with men. There is a reason the two are separated in the Shul and if you have questions, study the Torah. All you need is contained within."

Oh Julie, I wish I could talk to you and learn what is on the other side. Certainly there is life after death, but to what purpose is it all?

At the kitchen table Julie sat, still pondering the many things Baruk had said.

This apartment was a creation of his mind and thought; it was a memory that had meaning for him. Slowly, Julie remembered they had not lived here for nearly 20 years. He and Reba moved to the Projects in Williamsburg when their apartment on Union Avenue proved too expensive, not to mention it was difficult walking up two flights of stairs. Yet, Julie had chosen this place to awaken from the sleep of death.

Julie repeated to himself, so, I am dead. That pain in my stomach was the cause. If I had listened to Reba and gone to the doctors sooner, perhaps I would still be with her. She was right, I could not pray away all my aches and pains.

Julie got up and began walking around the apartment. While he was dead, he really didn't feel much different. Other than the terrible pain being gone, everything else seemed to be working the same. He walked over to the large mirror in the living room and looked at himself. His appearance seemed 30 years younger, as if he was 45. There was still some hair on his head, it was a little gray and his garb consisted of a white shirt with dark vest and pants. A black yarmulke was atop his head and he wore his favorite house slippers, the old brown ones.

Walking into the bedroom, it was the same way he remembered it; large double bed beside the window, a chest of drawers, and the freestanding wooden closet in the corner. Pictures of the family were on the wall, with Baruk's picture fixed between the bed and chest of drawers. Wait a second, Julie thought, Baruk's picture had changed; it was now empty. The frame was still there, but the picture itself was replaced with a gray emptiness. Julie stepped closer and, the more he stared into the picture, the more hypnotized he became by the gray backing; it was changing and in motion. The picture was empty, but alive with shifting textures of gray-like moving clouds. Somehow he knew Baruk's visit had altered the picture.

For a moment, Julie was frightened. Looking around the apartment, all the other pictures, except Sammy's, were gone. The apartment used to be filled with pictures of family and grandchildren; some on the furniture, some on the wall, some tucked into the mirror. Why, in this mental construct, had this changed?

Julie laughed to himself, thinking, I guess this thing will work itself out. If it is true, what Baruk said, this apartment is created by my soul so I can review my life and move on. The higher soul creates a reality to examine the meaningful portion of its life. The end result of this review is a decision about the next direction to travel. Ultimately, this decision is in accordance with the soul's own need for completion.

As Julie sat on his bed in his old apartment, he wondered why the Torah made no mention of this. Yet, the Torah spoke of a Judgment for all. Somehow all the good and evil that was done was recorded by angels and, on the Judgment Day, each soul would learn from God the Accounting. Yet, here it was different.

From Baruk's version, the higher soul recorded the life and, after a personal examination, rendered it's own accounting. The measure was service, learning and effort toward God. That part made sense; there was always a portion of Julie that knew the difference between right and wrong. It was that quiet voice that cautioned whenever he stepped too far over the line.

In the early years, when he drank excessively and chased everything in a skirt, Julie struggled to still that inner voice. No matter how hard he tried, even a wagon full of wine would not still it.

Julie was ashamed he couldn't be like the great man Baruk. So he turned the inner anger on himself and drank to hurt Baruk. Julie never realized Baruk never wanted his son to be like him; Baruk wanted Julie to be Julie, but Julie was too young and pig-headed to understand.

When Baruk urged Julie to work hard and apply himself to his studies, Baruk wasn't pointing out Julie's shortcomings. Baruk knew that preparation for life and work was essential. One day Julie would have to take care of a family and Baruk was fearful that Julie would not be prepared for this part of his life.

Finally, Julie realized that Baruk always loved and wanted the best for his son. Julie closed his eyes, focused inward, and muttered from deep within his soul, "Glory, glory be to God. You have always had my best interest at heart."

Julie found himself moving. He could see nothing and had no idea in which direction he traveled. The sensation was like his eyes were closed and he was being lead. He did not know how long he traveled but, suddenly, he was there.

Julie was on a street in lower Manhattan, outside the building where he used to work part-time as a tailor. A crowd of people had gathered in front of the building, looking down at something. As Julie felt the need to get inside to work, he pushed his way forward. Making his way through the layers of people, Julie overheard people repeating, "Who is he?" "Why did he do it?" "What a tragedy."

And as Julie grew closer, he saw the body of a fallen man. It was Moshe, who worked the sewing machine beside Julie. Moshe was lying on the ground bleeding, with his head split open; his body was broken and twisted in an unnatural way.

Julie called, "Moshe, what happened?" Immediately, one of the female bystanders replied, "You knew him? I saw it from across the street. It was terrible. He jumped . . . I saw him fall, then I screamed..."

Julie continued to stare down at Moshe. Then, in a flash, Julie found himself in another place. This place was indistinct and full of darkness. There was barely enough light to see. Next Julie heard a voice and slowly recognized that it belonged to Moshe. Julie strained to listen. What was Moshe saying?

"She doesn't love me. She doesn't love me. Then I don't want to live . . . I don't want to live . . ."

Listening closely, because it was difficult to see, Julie heard someone else reply, "You must leave this place and move on. Moshe, you must leave this place and move on."

Gradually, Julie realized he was listening to a conversation between Moshe and Others. In time, Julie adjusted to the darkness and saw who was speaking to Moshe. There were two beings present, mist-like in appearance, and attempting to comfort Moshe by projecting their Light toward him. Slowly, they would intensify and send illuminating energy into Moshe's darkness.

Over the next few minutes, the beings alternated between words of encouragement and transfer of Light. Throughout this time, Moshe repeated the refrain, "She doesn't love me. She doesn't love me."

Finally, Julie understood what he was watching. Moshe was locked into a place of darkness that he himself had created. This darkness caused him to end his own life. The two Beings of Light tried to help Moshe free himself from the dark world he created. In taking his life, Moshe sought to escape pain and darkness. His love had rejected him and he sought to end his suffering. Yet, he had taken the darkness with him and had not adjusted to the new place. Moshe was trapped in the past and the Beings of Light were trying to lead him forward.

Then Julie remembered his talk in the factory with Moshe as they both worked on pants and shirts. Moshe had fallen in love with one of the girls who stacked dresses. Sadly, she told him she felt nothing and her heart was given to another. This had been a year ago and Moshe could not get beyond it.

Julie counseled, the sea was filled with many fish and Moshe should go fishing for another. Moshe angrily replied that he could not do this and that Rebecca, which was the girl's name, was the only true love of his life. Julie warned that there were many like Rebecca and Moshe had to move on. This angered Moshe and he had never again spoken to Julie.

In this place, so far from the garment district, Moshe was still struggling to free himself of those painful feelings. He remained fixed in the same dark place. Sadly, Moshe's death had not provided release from his pain; he had learned nothing and taken pain with him. That was the tragedy.

Julie wondered, who were the beings that tried to help Moshe? Who were those healers of Light?

Again, Julie found himself seated on his bed, in his apartment, looking at the picture of Sammy on the wall. When this picture was taken, Sammy was six years old and climbing a tree. Sammy was the first grandchild and had been the joy of Julie's heart. All the attention he had not given to his own children – Laura, Judith and Larry – Julie gave the grandchildren.

By the time Sammy was born to Laura and her husband Joel, Julie was older and wiser. He worked to make up for his shortcomings as a father by being an attentive and loving grandfather. With Sammy, this was an opportunity to guide a little one.

With his own children, Julie had been distant and reluctant to give of himself. For the most part, Julie let Reba raise the three children, rarely showing interest in what they did. Julie's thoughts were on the injustices of his job and the struggle of his station in life. He had long ago given up the excesses of wine, but still had his eye on the occasional woman. The excitement of the chase and the conquest were empty solace for the pain and turmoil that was his inner life.

Then came Sammy. When Sammy was born, Julie made a vow to change. He became a loving grandfather and frequently attended the Shul to set an example for his grandson. Unable to find regular work, Julie spent many hours with Sammy. And, as the days turned into months, Sammy's life became Julie's joy; this joy filled Julie and he gave up his bad habits and even found peace in the Torah.

In time, Julie realized that the love he had in his heart for Sammy was a small piece of the infinite love God had in his heart for Julie. And, if God could love Julie with all his faults, then it was Julie's duty to live a good and honorable life.

Laura's apartment was around the corner from the apartment on Union Avenue, and a day did not go by when Julie did not visit his grandson. In caring for Sammy, Julie was trying to atone for all the bad things he had done; he was reaching higher.

Sammy was Julie's chance to find the meaning and joy in life. Proudly, Julie took Sammy to the park and on walks around the neighborhood. Julie helped sew and craft Sammy's clothing by making use of his skills as a tailor. For the six years Sammy was alive, Julie's heart was filled with joy and pride and love.

Then came the winter of 1948 and the terrible pneumonia outbreak. One cold night in February, Joel summoned Julie to Sammy's bedside. The doctor had been called and treatment prescribed, but still the fever raged; by the hour, Sammy grew weaker.

Laura and Joel spoke to the Rabbi who said to gather the men and pray. Often the prayers of the faithful were granted and, as God willed, Sammy might be saved. So, the men gathered in Laura's apartment and implored the Father to cure the innocent child.

While the men prayed, still the fever raged and the more they prayed, the quicker Sammy slipped away. As it reached 9 p.m., mercifully, Sammy was taken; his heart stopped beating and, slowly, his fever-drained body grew cold. As Laura looked from her dead son to outside the bedroom window, she saw grandfather Baruk's smiling face appear in the darkness. Baruk's face was aglow with kindness, love, and sympathy. He whispered to Laura not to worry, for Sammy was with God.

Around the corner, on Union Avenue, Reba paced, worried about her grandson. As the clock in the living room struck 9 p.m., she heard a crash in the bedroom. Quickly, Reba ran into the bedroom to see what had fallen; Sammy's picture lay on the floor. The glass was broken and Reba realized that Sammy had passed. He had fallen from the tree of life. It was the same picture that hung on the bedroom wall.

While Julie reminisced about his first grandson, there came ringing of the apartment doorbell. As Julie went to see who was calling, he realized he had not thought of that cold winter night in nearly 27 years. Julie had locked that part of himself away; it was too painful to remember.

Slowly, Julie walked through the kitchen and, hesitantly, reached for the doorknob. He was afraid of what might be on the other side. Yet, he remembered that this entire situation, this creation, was for him. Somehow his mind and the forces of the universe were creating this reality, so that in death Julie might review the important parts of his life. Through this process, he would learn and move on. What was there to be afraid of? All of this was a part of his life and he had already lived it.

Julie opened the door. Standing there, in the hallway was Sammy, appearing exactly as he did at six years old. Sammy reached out, smiled and said, "Daddy dropped me off downstairs. He said I was old enough to come up by myself. Gompa, I am here for a visit."

Julie staggered and held onto the doorknob for support; he almost fell from the shock of seeing his grandson. It was like time had stood still and pneumonia had never drained the child's fragile body. Julie reached and picked Sammy up, hugging Sammy to his chest and kissed him on the cheek.

"Come on Sammy, I have some candies for you." Carrying Sammy into the living room, Julie put him down on the sofa and reached into the candy dish on the table for two jelly candies. Somehow Julie knew the candies would be there and, as his mind whirled from the excitement, he was grateful to be with his grandson again. Julie lovingly looked at Sammy thinking, this dying is not so bad. At least I have Sammy for company.

Sammy sat on the sofa beside Julie, who wondered why Sammy hadn't removed the wrapper and eaten one of the candies. As though reading his mind, Sammy spoke, "Gompa, it is not permitted to eat the candy. I have come for a brief visit to tell you something. Then I must leave."

"What is that," said Julie, "you cannot stay?"

"No Gompa; it is not permitted."

"Sammy, why have you come?"

"To tell you, God loves you and always has. You were wrong to blame yourself. I did not die, Gompa, because you were bad. I died from the fever because it was time. Everyone was to learn from my passing."

Sammy leaned over on the sofa and kissed Julie on the cheek. Julie imagined he could almost feel Sammy's warm skin.

"Gompa, I have to go now. Soon we will see each other again. Later, when you have left Union Avenue." Slowly, Sammy began to fade and was gone.

Immediately after Sammy's departure, Julie began to weep and called out to God, "Oh Father, why do you continue to hurt me so?"

After a time, Julie pulled himself together and began to think further about the place that he was in and the process he was undergoing. Baruk indicated the review of Julie's life was necessary so that something else might happen. Wondering what this might be, he walked into the bedroom and looked for Sammy's picture on the wall; it was gone.

This made Julie nervous and he began to pace. As he paced, Julie continued to think about Baruk and Sammy's visits and what it was like to be dead. "Yes, the great ones were right; there is an existence after leaving the body. It is a multiple leveled existence of mind and thought. After the physical passing, there is time to reflect, learn and pause. Then it is time to move on. But move on to what?"

Julie realized he would have to wait to find out.

Again, Julie found himself traveling. This time the motion was downward. Like the previous experience, Julie could not see anything; he just felt movement and direction.

In a matter of moments, Julie was able to see and found himself in Esther's house. He was standing beside Reba, who was unaware that he was there. As Julie searched the living room, he saw most of his family sitting Shiva on old wooden crates and chairs. In the center of the room was a Being of Light, emitting love, peace, and energy to everyone present. Julie could feel the loving peace and see the beams of Light connecting with the souls of different family members. Somehow, the Being of Light was pulling the energy from the air and reflecting the healing rays to each person. While this Being of Light was part of the very fabric of the air, it was separate as well.

As Julie wondered about the Being of Light, an answer to Julie's question formed in his mind. "I am what you have called a guardian angel. During this difficult time, I am here to help Reba and the others. They cannot see me. I am here to help ease their pain."

Then, in an instant, Julie felt himself moving; he was traveling upward and, before he had time to think about anything, he found himself sitting again at his kitchen table on Union Avenue. Resting there, Julie began to think about Reba and what a good friend, mother and wife she had been.

Clearly, of the two of them, she was the better person, with the kinder heart. Always Reba thought about other people and did the right thing; Julie was selfish. Throughout their lives together, Julie had often fallen short of the mark, putting his needs before the needs of family. Not Reba; she was born with an inner sense of goodness and knew what to do. In their religion, women were called the weaker vessel. Between the two of them, he had fallen many times and Reba was always there to pick him up.

Until he met Reba, it had been difficult for Julie to love. They had met at a social function run by the Shul. As immigrants settled on the lower eastside of Manhattan, family introduced the newcomer to

American ways and the Shul was the center of life. Here, even more than in the old country, the Shul was the basis by which people became part of the community. In the ceremonies, the old ways were kept and people met others who were struggling to learn the ways of a new country.

Unlike Julie, Reba had traveled to America with a family member, her aunt. Reba's parents, who Julie never met, owned an inn and restaurant in Russia. The Czar and his Cossacks were seizing property and killing all witnesses. Reba's parents were reluctant to leave everything they had worked for years to build. However, they did not want to take a chance with their daughter's life and sent her to America with a chaperone. In time, Reba's parents were killed and their land taken by an officer in the Russian Army.

Often, to stay in the old country meant loss of property and death. Coming to America provided the opportunity for life and a new start. Julie's own father, Baruk, saw the oppression coming and chose to stay behind. Early on, Baruk had given to the poor and, as things grew worse, gave away all his possessions and land. For Baruk, this was preferable to the government taking over what he worked to accumulate. Like so many others, Baruk was slain by the Cossacks. Julie learned of his father's death through a cousin who barely escaped with his own life.

As Julie sat in their apartment, he wondered if Reba were here now, what she would say. Julie realized he had unfinished business with Reba; he had hurt her many times and never asked for her forgiveness.

In the early years, he shut Reba out and never shared the painful darkness that would overtake him. Perhaps, if he had discussed with Reba his inner demons and fears, he might not have needed to suffer so much. When the inner pain overtook him, the only peace was the haze of wine and the tavern's gaiety. For a time, this excitement and pleasure drove away the pain, but always the darkness returned.

Eventually, Julie's health began to fail and he gave up wine. It rotted away his stomach and all that was left to kill the emotional pain was the excitement of an affair. In time, this too passed. When Sammy was born, Julie promised to be a good example for his grandson; magically, the time spent with Sammy chased away the darkness and emotional pain Julie felt about not being good enough.

After Sammy's death, Julie became distant and took to praying long hours. Julie was convinced that God punished him because of the immoral way he lived his life. Now all of this was proven untrue. Oh, why had he taken the easy way and allowed so many things to stand between himself and Reba?

Then, Julie fell to his knees and called out, "Oh Reba, I wish I had learned to share my pain and joy. My own darkness and selfish desire kept me from being a better husband and friend. I love you for all you have given me. Please forgive me . . ."

In the place where time stands still, the place where that which is Timeless enters and manifests, the Guardians monitored the coming and going of souls. It was, and is, in this place that the Universal Mind entwines with the destiny of souls. It is here that the Universal Plan aligns with each soul's individual destiny.

The Guardians watched as Julie's soul worked out its next step along the path to completion and return to the Timeless. The Guardians waited as Julie called himself to judgment and, when the time was right, the Guardians would act in accordance with the Timeless Plan.

Reba found herself breaking into a cold sweat. For an instant, she felt as if Julie were in the room beside her. Needing fresh air, Reba went outside into the backyard for a few moments to be alone.

Reba thought, it is good to be outside and feel the warm sunlight on my face. She was growing impatient for the mourning period to end, so she could return to her own apartment, free to do whatever she wanted. It would be lonely without Julie, but in their 45 years together, there were many times she was lonely with him.

Julie had been a difficult man to get to know; his dark moods made him quiet and distant. Reba realized Julie was a man that didn't like himself and this self-hatred often put a wall between him and others. Julie never felt his father loved him, but Reba knew it was Julie who had difficulty loving himself.

Yet, there had also been wonderful times. Often Julie was aglow with the accomplishments of his grandchildren. Time and age had mellowed Julie. He was a much better grandfather than he was a father.

Even with all his faults, Reba loved Julie. She loved the way, as he grew older, he offered to make her tea and cook for the grandchildren. He was a terrible cook but he tried to please and Reba loved that about him.

It was difficult when she learned of his affairs and threw him out of the apartment. Always she took him back; the children needed a father and she needed Julie. Who could explain love? Julie was the little boy who wouldn't grow up.

Fortunately, like a good wine, Julie improved with age. In time, he abandoned his excesses, finding comfort in the world of the Shul. He was the prodigal child and the Rabbi's son found peace in the prayer shawl and yarmulke.

It was their quiet mornings together that Reba would miss the most. The hours before Julie's trip to the Shul and before she would go outside to sit on the benches to listen to the other women's problems. Daily, Reba and Julie set aside this special time to have breakfast. Often they sat quietly eating, still in love with each other.

Somehow, the years taught them how to accept each other's shortcomings and to celebrate the small joys of life. Both had come to a new country with little money and raised three children who, in time, provided them with eight grandchildren. Surely there had been many tears, but there had also been laughter and a loving family.

When Reba returned to her apartment and the outdoor benches, it would now be time for the women to listen to her problems. The cup of suffering had been passed.

Julie rested in his easy chair and considered all that had happened. Being dead, in many ways, was like being alive, except that there was no weight to the body. While he appeared the same physically, body sensations, like pain and excitement, were much fainter. Sometimes he still felt hungry but he was never tired from exertion. Also, while he needed to sleep, it was not from physical activity. The work and activity in this place was primarily emotional and spiritual. Here, the use of his mind made him tired.

For the most part, the events that were taking place were those that occurred during his life. He was reviewing and evaluating past experience. Yet, he remained unsure as to the criteria or yardstick against which he should judge. Why was he going over these specific events and what was he supposed to learn?

Then there were the mysterious trips to locations and places where different spiritual activity was taking place. Clearly, this place had many levels to it. The review of his life seemed to be part of a larger activity. Baruk had indicated that Julie's higher soul was controlling what took place in this location. Were there other locations besides this one? Where was heaven and hell? Was his higher soul connected to other locations?

As Julie thought about these things, he wondered how this self-evaluation was related to the biblical final judgment and accounting. In the traditional narration, in both the Old and New Testaments, God would do the final accounting and it would be collective for all souls. Was this Day of Judgment in addition to the individual sorting out that Julie was doing? Were these two judgments related in some way, and in the process, was each soul to contribute?

Inwardly, Julie realized all of this was connected or it would not be happening. What was the next step? As Julie wondered about this, he found his lips repeating the first commandment, "Thou shall love, honor, and serve thy Lord, thy God with all thy heart and soul." Julie spoke these words slowly and with reverence. Here, in this place, the words were filled with Light and love and hope.

Julie found himself sitting in the old Shul on Union Avenue. This was the converted church that his congregation had purchased to keep their traditions. In the beginning, Julie had felt uncomfortable; for 50 years it had been a church where Christians prayed. The Greek Orthodox Church had sold it because their numbers in the community declined. The old Rabbi said that their congregation was fortunate to have found this place. The price was good and it had been God's House for many years.

It took a long time for Julie to accept this view. Finally, he realized that Jesus was a Jew and, as long as Julie remembered this, it helped. Often Julie wondered how Baruk would have accepted praying in what had been a holy house for Christians. Yet, when Julie thought about these concerns now, they seemed to be of little importance. In the afterlife, the tension between Christians and Jews

155

was unimportant. The house was God's House, just like the old Rabbi said.

But, what of the other beliefs that Julie held about God and religion? Did these things also fade in the afterlife? So far, all that Julie had seen of God was the loving Light that gave everything its form and substance.

Julie laughed when he thought about how he feared man's flight into space. Almost fanatically, Julie believed that it was an insult to God, like the Tower of Babel, to travel into the heavens. When the spacecraft journeyed into God's realm, Julie believed that God would destroy the earth, that God would strike out against man's blasphemy and destroy those who sought to travel to heaven in their physical body.

When Julie reluctantly watched on television the takeoff and landing, he believed the Devil was creating an illusion to fool and tempt the righteous. For months, Julie walked around, waiting for the destruction. When pictures of the earth from space were shown in the newspapers, Julie was suspicious. To him, the earth looked like a colored ball and felt the Devil was trying to fool the faithful.

Yet, Julie was dead and was not in heaven or the other place either. Julie's religious views had not prepared him for this and this made him uncomfortable. He began to worry. Baruk had said that this place, this reality, was created by Julie's own soul so that he could examine what needed to be examined. Hopefully, Julie would learn what he had to learn and move on. That was the point of this place.

This place was created by his higher soul so he might benefit. This was all in accord with the Divine Plan. Clearly, this place was not hell and Julie figured it was not heaven either.

And, as Julie continued to think about his life, he wondered how his long hours of prayer, in this old Shul, had prepared him for this place. What yardstick had he been given to sort this out?

Then, Julie found himself repeating the first commandment, "Thou shall love, honor, and serve thy Lord, thy God with all thy heart and soul."

Continuing to sit in the old Shul, Julie thought about his life. What had he learned? Over the years, how had he served God? What had he given to others?

Then, in a flash, memories began to flood into Julie's mind. It had not all been a life of selfishness. He had served and given his love. That was what God wanted, unselfish love to others. Gradually, a smile came across Julie's face as he remembered Michael's Bar Mitzvah. Yes, that was a wonderful hour.

Julie remembered the night when Larry, his son, called. Larry was upset because Michael, his eldest, was having trouble with his Bar Mitzvah teacher and lesson. When Larry went to speak with the teacher, they both argued and now Michael had no place to have his Bar Mitzvah.

Julie reassured Larry that everything would work out and asked him more about the problem. In order to receive his Bar Mitzvah, Michael had to practice singing his lesson using a recording made by the teacher and to play the recording, they needed to buy a record player. Larry barely had enough money for the lessons and donation to the Shul.

When Larry went to discuss this problem with the teacher, the teacher insisted this was the way the lesson had to be taught. Michael needed to practice with the recording on his own so that when he met weekly with the teacher, they could refine the musical presentation. The teacher said this was the way he taught; no recording, no lessons, no Bar Mitzvah. It worked this way because he was the only teacher in their Shul. If Larry wanted his son to have a traditional ceremony and sing in front of the whole congregation on Saturday morning, he had to do it the teacher's way. This attitude made Larry furious and he told the teacher, even if he could somehow borrow the money, he didn't want Michael to be taught by such a closed minded person.

Now what were they going to do? How was Michael going to have his Bar Mitzvah and stand before God as a man? There was not enough time to find another teacher or Shul. Could Julie help?

Again, Julie reassured Larry and told him not to worry. Michael would have a Bar Mitzvah. Julie arranged to have Michael's Bar Mitzvah during the week in the Shul on Union Avenue. During the week, Michael had to sing three blessings that he already knew. Larry did not have to pay for lessons or expensive equipment that he could not afford. On Saturday they could have a party for everyone to attend.

As Julie remembered this event, he wondered why it was coming back to him. What was so special about it? All he did was help his son and grandson with a problem. It was not even a difficult problem. All Julie had to do was speak to the old Rabbi at their Shul; it was he that suggested this course of action. The Rabbi was honored to be of help.

Julie thought more about this event and his grandson's face appeared. Michael was now a grown man and he spoke to Julie. "Grandpa, what you did was one of the kindest things ever done for me. Thank you."

Julie replied, "You do not have to thank me for arranging the Bar Mitzvah, I was happy to do it."

"No Grandpa," said Michael, "the Bar Mitzvah was beautiful and I was worried that I would not have one, but the special part was after the ceremony."

"You mean, the party at Gluckstern's on Saturday?"

"No Grandpa, when you took me to the movie on Thursday afternoon; the rock-and-roll movie. That was the special part. It was one of the kindest things anyone has ever done for me."

"How can taking you to a movie be the kindest thing anyone has ever done for you? I do not understand?"

"Well, you see Grandpa, after the ceremony when we were in the Shul, you said, what would you like to do today? Larry has to go to work and will not be back until 5 p.m. to get you. We have the whole day together and you can pick what you want to do.

"I said, let's go see the new rock and roll movie. You said fine and, after we went back to the apartment to see Grandma Reba, we went to the movie in downtown Brooklyn. Throughout the entire movie, you just sat there smiling and enjoyed just being with me.

"It was not until many years later that I realized, as an Orthodox Jew, going to this movie was a very difficult thing for you to do. It was against your religious belief to watch a rock-and-roll movie, yet you did it with joy. That was the special act of kindness I never forgot."

This brought a tear to Julie's eye and an ache to his heart. As he thought deeply about what his grandson said, Larry's face now appeared before Julie.

"Papa, the Bar Mitzvah was a special day for me too. That night, when I called for help, I fully expected you to give me the money for the record player and recording. I never expected you to open your heart to us in that way. You offered more than money; you made our problem, your problem and as a family, we solved it.

"What you were not able to give as I was growing up, you provided to my son. In this way, the love extended across the years and washed away tears of pain between us.

"I love you Papa." With those words, Larry disappeared.

Julie closed his eyes and began to cry.

Slowly, Julie began to pull himself together and remembered a story one of the Rabbis told.

There once was a young man who was traveling on a hot, dusty road. As he walked, he wished there were some shade he could rest beneath. Walking on a little further, he stepped upon a seed that had fallen. It had slipped from the pack of a passing traveler. He picked the seed up and tossed it into the tall grass that lined the road. He hoped, in the years to come, this seed would grow into a tree that would provide shade and comfort for others.

And as the years passed, an orchard grew from this tiny seed. Thousands of travelers have been able to gain rest and comfort from this singular act of kindness performed by a traveler long forgotten.

When the Rabbi concluded the story he said, "It was this one act of charity that raised the traveler into heaven. God's Mercy exceeds His Wrath tenfold."

At the time, Julie could not understand the story. He thought the old one was repeating something that sounded good, but had little practical meaning. Yet, Julie never realized that sitting through the rock-and-roll movie, which he hated, had affected his grandson that much. Or that Larry felt so strongly about Julie's participation in the Bar Mitzvah. Julie had only done what any grandfather would have been pleased to do; he helped his son and grandson arrange the traditional rite of passage.

Who could measure the effect of an event? Or the outcome of a life?

159

Julie was again traveling downward and found himself standing on a street corner in lower Manhattan. As he waited for the streetlight to change, Julie looked to his left and saw an elderly woman step out to cross the street.

The light was still green and Julie called to the woman who was now in danger from speeding cars, "Stop! Don't cross!" Unfortunately, she could not hear and continued crossing. Fearfully, Julie watched as a truck came roaring down the road, jamming on the brakes as it hit and instantly killed the old woman.

Horrified, Julie watched as bystanders began to gather and tried to assist the fallen woman. Then, Julie saw the woman's soul slowly leave her crushed body and begin to rise. In an instant, a being of pure, white Light appeared to help the disoriented woman travel upward. The Being of Light extended a helping hand and in a soft, kind, voice said, "I am here to help you journey on. Please, take my hand and I will lead you up."

Julie saw both the Being of Light and the woman's soul traveling hand in hand toward the heavens.

IV - An Enriching Element

Much time had passed and Julie spent it reviewing different events in his life, traveling to places on the earth and in the afterlife. All of these experiences, memories, and journeys were offered to help him reflect upon what he had done in relation to what he wished to become.

This process of learning and developing cosmic potential was in relation to the service Julie chose to provide. The Guardians constantly monitored the interconnectedness of needs and factors. In the Timeless Place, where all things created and yet-to-be are aligned, these celestial beings bind and set free, according to the ongoing Plan. The universe and all things are evolving to a higher condition. These hidden Guardians are the protectors of the Plan.

The Universal Mind, or Source, originates in a place beyond the Guardians. This place is as distant from the Guardians as the Guardians are distant from Julie. Yet, these distances, while seemingly far, are really close. For the interconnectedness is Divine, as the parent is always part of the child.

The Guardians monitored Julie's progress and the progress of all souls; this is their charge and responsibility. Julie had grown and reviewed many of the events of his life, but had not uncovered the benchmark or measure by which they were to be viewed. He was growing closer and now it was time for an enriching element. A nutrient was to be added.

When Julie opened his eyes, he found himself seated on a mountain, atop a serene pastoral setting overlooking a wide valley. About him were four other students. Each was resplendent in Light; Julie was also adorned in Light and his intensity was the same as the others. These beings were no longer shaped like humans, but were configurations of Light that approximated what they had once been like in the physical.

Each of the four beings vibrated at the same intensity as Julie and were seated in front of the teacher. The teacher was of a higher order and vibrated at a much finer intensity; his Light was a rare blue-white.

All present were filled with love, peace, and happiness. Here, in this place, communication was through thought and energy; words were replaced by unspoken energy patterns and images projected mind-to-mind.

The teacher, or Being of Light, was able to communicate simultaneously with each of the five students, who were advancing in their capacity to use the spiritual dimension. Each worked and learned at their own pace, but all were ready for the next phase in evolution. The progress was individual and in accordance with the Plan projected through the Guardians. Each soul has a place in this Plan, contributing to the emerging design, spiraling upward and back to our original home. In this grand Plan, the Guardians and Beings of Light protect us from our own selfish desires and destruction.

Before any can evolve and take the next step, they must pass through this station. Located on this mountain, in this place and time, exists a cosmic classroom. Learning is offered to enhance individual capacity for knowledge and service.

The Universal Mind, or Creator, gave life to the universe so that He might be known and, when known, be loved. Along with this knowledge and love comes service and Light. This is the Plan. This is the evolution that the Guardians and Beings of Light reflect, cherish and maintain. This was the cosmic energy force that projected itself throughout the universe. This is the rare nectar that Julie sipped.

The Being of Light projected, to each of the five students, questions and probes that were individually designed. During the exchange, Julie was unaware of their individual answers, yet could sense the simultaneous participation of the others.

The Being asked of Julie, "So, what have you learned?"

Julie replied, "After the passing of the body, there is another beginning. One phase ends and another begins. I am tied to that person I was. I carry with me the joy, triumph and failure of that experience, but there are other dimensions to travel and we journey through love.

"The universe is a vast expanse and I am a ray of light from a much larger sun. Its brilliance shelters me and, in the earth phase, asks what I did to honor its grandeur. Love and giving require the right action and purpose. As the great ones taught, you can only take with you to the next place your good actions; these are of Light and love."

As Julie sat waiting for a response, he felt energy, Light and love pass between them all. On this energy was the meaning of things and the answer to every question. This energy was the Universal Mind, or Source, and their replies were part of this energy.

"Who was Julie?" the Being questioned.

"Julie was, and is, a being of many layers; each was required for the earth phase. These were subject to variations in time and place and formed his makeup. Yet, while these were necessary for daily life, there was another part of Julie that was timeless. The point of the earth phase is to use individual talents to make things better. Each is a timeless ray of Light and each is a piece of the Creator. In the earth phase, we share the opportunity with others to celebrate and reach higher toward our ultimate cosmic potential. Each individual has a potential and as rays of Light will return to the larger sun.

"Most of my life I sought momentary pleasure and tried to exert my will on the situation. I forgot the higher call and how we are all connected in the brilliance of the Light. Most of my hours I spent in pleasure, cutting myself off from others and my own inner spark."

The Being again queried, "So, what have you learned?"

Julie paused for a moment, trying to go deeper. It was the same question now for a second time and he searched for more to say. Then Julie remembered. "In each life, there are opportunities to grow closer to our lasting self. These opportunities, or events, are the coming together of many factors, and we are presented with the potential to exert our higher will on the situation. Do we act based upon what our lower nature wants for itself or do we act in accordance with the higher element? This higher element, or spark of Light, is that which leads us from realm to realm. This moment of service to help another reach upward, ultimately, is the purpose of life. For this higher action is what we take with us and helps prepare us for this realm.

"Since my passing, I have learned that both realms are filled with joyous elements. Each abounds with wonders and we connect with our higher nature when we are one with the Light. In the earth phase, I hurt many with my selfish and stubborn nature. In most situations, I thought that I knew best. As I have traveled far from that land and had time to reflect, I see that many of my actions missed the mark. Mostly I hurt those closest to me because I sought my needs, not the higher.

"Yet, there were times when I aligned with the higher. These came later, as the oil ran low in the lamp."

The Being questioned further, "Who was Julie?"

"Julie was the son of Baruk, born in a small village in eastern Russia. His mother died birthing him. Julie was a Rabbi's son who knew that he could never wear the robes of his father, so he struck out in anger and self-destruction. Sadly, Julie realized too late that all he had to be was Julie. No one expected another Baruk; the universe needed Julie, but Julie was slow in opening to the sun. His early years were filled with bitterness and self-loathing, yet, beneath that exterior, was a Being of Light waiting to shine. And, as Julie learned to share this inner spark and love with his grandchildren, Julie became that which he was created to be. Julie became a better husband, father, and grandfather. It was love that set Julie free; fortunately, he learned this before it was time to leave.

"The scriptures and wise ones were right about this part; all are Beings of Light that come into the earth phase to love and work and serve. When our time is up we travel to another place, taking with us all that we created. Oh, that my load was lighter! I wish that I had worried less and loved more. I wish that I had spent less time thinking about my needs and played more with my children and grandchildren. I wish that I had shared more time with Reba and talked about her needs instead of selfishly praying each morning in the Shul. It was not those prayers that brought me closer to who I was; it was my time with Reba, gently sharing our life together.

"Who was Julie? What did he learn? Julie was a man like other men.

"He sought what he wanted when he wanted it; just like other men. In his passing, Julie learned that this part was only the surface. Julie was made up of many layers and had places inside himself that he never went. These places were filled with hidden treasures and the secret to life. Yes, Julie was many things but he learned to look deeper late in the game. He should have traveled to all the parts of himself instead of staying only on the shore. The shore was the surface of Julie, not the magical Julie. Service to others meant listening to them and giving what they needed. In the evening of his life, Julie learned to love and serve. If he had found this sooner, how much finer it would have been for him and those he loved. Think of all the benefits, if this love and service had been discovered in the early years."

Julie rested. He looked out from the high mountain peak, thinking that this realm was similar to the earth. Some of the constructs, places and beings were images of the world he had left behind.

Here, in this place, it was a realm of thought and spirit. Consciousness, or energy, was the basis of things. The mountain he was sitting upon was consciousness. Unlike those on earth – which were made of stone, grass and dirt – this peak was a projection of mind. Assembled in this location were the beings that needed to partake in the exchange. Each was an individual and the location was a construct or idea they shared. Maybe it was something only Julie experienced. In the time Julie had been on this side, he realized that the universe was, in many ways, a construct of mind. Of course there was a larger reality, but the reality one experienced often depended upon one's own consciousness.

Was Julie really on this mountain with four other beings learning about the past and future? Questions like this no longer troubled Julie. Julie had learned to go deeper into things and experience the Light. For in the Light was the timeless essence that was Julie's home, and the pure being that sat with them emanated this Light. Light was the Life Force, the mother and father of everyone, and all knowing and pure love. This Julie was certain about; just as he was certain he left the earth phase to travel to this one.

As Reba sat on the bench outside her apartment, in the housing project, she enjoyed the late morning sun against her face. Julie had been dead now for months and, as was their custom, Reba continued to wear widow's black.

During their years together, Reba had forgiven Julie for many things. She forgave his stubbornness, his habits of excess, and his seeming indifference to their children . . . but it had been difficult to forgive his refusal to go to the doctor. Julie wanted things his own way and that was why he was not there with her.

Certainly, as the years passed and Julie grew older, he slowed down and most of his faults fell away. Gradually, he tried to help Reba around the apartment and even went shopping for groceries with her. Then Julie took more interest in their children, particularly as the grandchildren came along. Julie was a good grandfather and enjoyed the Sunday family visits. It had been years since Julie lived the tavern life. Julie said that God had warned him not to continue with it. Reba never pushed the subject, grateful to have Julie for herself.

Yet, Reba was having trouble forgiving Julie's neglect of his health. Julie was her best friend and showed little concern for her by not going to the doctor sooner. Perhaps, if he had gotten timely care, Julie might be sitting with her and enjoying the late morning sun.

As Julie traveled with the other students on the Light of the universe, reflected by the Being of Light, he was filled with Oneness. In that moment, Julie was One with everything and experienced the Divine connection. In both worlds, this spiritual One-ness was the basic structure of things. It was the link between the living and the dead; everyone was connected by this loving, peaceful energy.

Meditating with his eyes closed, Julie continued to bathe in celestial bliss and he wondered, is this loving, peaceful energy God?

Suddenly, a wave of knowing energy was directed toward Julie and the answer came. It traveled on another caress of spiritual ecstasy, "This is but a small taste of things to come."

This caress overwhelmed Julie and he had to open his eyes. Surprisingly, he found himself standing in a field of wild flowers. It was a clear fall day and there was a gentle breeze blowing across the meadow. Brilliant colors – purple, yellow, green – danced in the sunlight. Julie breathed the clear air, smelled the perfumed fragrance of the flowers, felt the sun on his face, hearing the words, "So, what have you learned?"

Again, this question caused Julie to pause and reflect. Was the Being of Light referring to his life, the journey into the afterlife, or to the meadow of flowers around him? To what was the Master referring?

And again, Julie heard the inner question; the insistence required an answer.

Gazing at the purple and yellow flowers as they danced on the wind, spontaneously Julie replied, "This beauty, this interconnectedness, all sings the praise of the Creator. Like the wild flowers, we are always in the Creator's heart and the Creator has a plan for each. The song of life and existence must arise from deep within and within each is a unique melody.

"We travel through the universe singing this song and creating, in our own individual way, a small world. We are always connected to the life force, the creative energy, and are most lost when we forget this. The darkness of our inner fears can only be stilled by the Light of knowledge and love."

Julie found himself seated in one of the pews in the old Shul on Union Avenue. As he looked about, he saw that he was the only person present; the Shul was empty. Julie was seated directly before the Arc which held the Torah that, according to tradition, was closed.

Julie looked up toward the balcony and saw the closed curtain, or veil, where the women sat during service. The balcony was as quiet as the old Shul, and Julie drank in the peacefulness. It had taken Julie a lifetime to be able to sit in the Shul and not be filled with guilt about the way he acted toward his father.

Then, as Julie continued to absorb the stillness about him, he was stirred by the inner command, "So, what have you learned?"

By this time Julie realized he could not resist and spontaneously began to answer. "All those years I ran from God, I was running from myself. God is not found in Shul or church, God is within each of us. All are children of the Light and carry within a divine spark. This spark is our compass and serves to guide us through the many worlds. It is our port in the stormy night and the island from which we come forth renewed and ready to journey on. The Shul represents our body and the Torah represents our connection to the Divine. The doors of the Ark must be opened within each. What makes the Shul holy is not the scripture, but the purity of heart of the worshipper. The curtain that separates the women from the men is the veil of selfishness that separates our worldly-self from the Divine spark within.

"Each is sent into the physical world with an opportunity to serve. Like the One who gave us life, we too can be Lords of Creation and make the world a better, more loving place. As we connect with our higher self, we connect with the Light and live each moment for God.

"Daily, I went to Shul looking for God, yet God was waiting for me long before I went looking. God was waiting in the quiet of my heart."

Julie was traveling, soaring through space. When he stopped, he found himself in a graveyard. Gazing about, he saw hundreds of headstones and curiously he started to read some of the names. After reading a few of the closest, he realized that he was in a Jewish graveyard and tradition forbade, as a Kohane, that he stand there.

Feeling something behind him, he turned to see what was making him feel uncomfortable. Quickly, he noticed a plot that had recently been filled. The ground was high, not having time to settle, and grass had not completely grown. Also, as a year had not passed, there was no head stone. Slowly, Julie recognized the location and realized this was his grave and the empty space alongside waited for his beloved, Reba.

Standing by his grave, knowing that part of him rested in the soil made Julie sad. And, as he stood motionless, not knowing what to do or say, Julie heard the inner command, "So, what have you learned?"

Fighting back tears and not wanting to answer, Julie hesitated. Yet, the inner voice was unrelenting and called again, "So, what have you learned?"

Speaking in a low voice as a tear came down his cheek, Julie replied, "Our hours in this world are like an afternoon in the sun. Like the wild flowers that dance in the meadow, we are here for a brief moment in the timeless eternity. It is important what we do and how we live. Yet, if we have not connected with our higher nature, we are like ships that are adrift on the water without a rudder. Each has talents and abilities that are to be used to enrich the world. We were sent into this world as emissaries of the Light and are to join with our family and friends in the timeless celebration that is all around us.

"This world is also filled with darkness, suffering, and tears. Yet, man creates most of the suffering. Man is made in the image of God and has unlimited creative potential. This potential can be channeled toward the Light or toward the darkness; this is the struggle within each. Do we turn toward the darkness, our selfish desires that harm others, or toward the Light and a higher call?

"One day each returns to the earth. Yet, there are other worlds, other experiences, and other opportunities. For the Father is all loving.

"It is only a fool that squanders his birthright. We are all born children of a king and become lost, broken, and afraid when we forget our heritage. Each has a divine spark within and this spark will lead us, through the many worlds, back to our Father."

As Julie closed his eyes and slowly repeated the Name of God, he was no longer tearful and afraid. Spiritually, he was home and at peace.

This time when Julie opened his eyes, he found himself in a great hall with a high ceiling and many adjoining rooms. The entire structure was constructed of Light and Julie was standing next to the Being of Light and the other students.

The great hall seemed to go on forever and, in every room that Julie looked, he saw scrolls of written records. The records were neatly stacked on shelves and appeared to be placed in order. Each room, each stack of scrolls, emanated with Light; the Light was in different hues and seemed to come from the scrolls themselves.

The overall effect and radiance of the great hall was a peaceful, golden hue. As Julie looked further, and his eyes adapted to the varying intensity of light, he saw that the individual rooms were without doors. And each room, while filled with scrolls of many colors and hues, had a specific overall radiance. There were some rooms that glistened in yellow, white, and orange light. Other rooms radiated blue, black, and green. Light was everywhere and throughout the rooms, all the colors of the spectrum were represented in a rainbow of colors.

Gazing up, Julie perceived deep stillness. This stillness, while profound and ancient, permeated with energy, wisdom, and love. It was from this high center that Julie realized the direction and order of the great hall originated.

As Julie enjoyed the beauty and harmony of this wonderful place, he perceived the Being of Light address the five students. "We are allowed only a brief glimpse of this place. This is the great hall of records and each scroll represents a life, an opportunity to learn and work and serve. Then, each soul moves forward. This hall extends far into the past and into the distant future. Each room is a different world with endless possibilities. The Guardians and their servants, the Masters of Reincarnation, oversee all of this. All serve the higher law and reside above in the timeless stillness.

"The universe and countless worlds are all evolving upward, toward completion. The great plan serves the Creator, spiraling, whirling toward home. The point of all creation is to experience and serve, returning in partnership with God. That is the soul's journey."

V - Three Events

More time had passed. Julie was resting in his easy chair in the apartment on Union Avenue, thinking about the classroom with the Being of Light and students. Never getting a chance to communicate with the others, he wondered about them. Had they recently passed into the next world, and were they also getting instruction and gaining awareness of their surroundings? Julie could not be sure; he never heard their lessons, understanding that the learning was both individual and collective among the five.

Suddenly, Julie heard the apartment doorbell ring. Rising to open the door, Julie became nervous. From experience, he had learned that on this side you could never be sure who or what was calling.

Julie reached and opened the door. Standing before him was the Being of Light. Shining in his robe of Light, he radiated a loving, peaceful energy. The Master's sudden appearance at Julie's door was surprising. Why had the Master waited for Julie to open the door? Surely, with his power, the Master could have entered with or without Julie's permission.

Then, Julie remembered this entire world was a series of mental images. Extensions of mind, which when properly directed, changed at a moment's notice. If the Master had wished, he could have entered Julie's apartment without stopping at the door.

Yet, the Master waited. Julie inquired, "Holy one, why are you at my door?"

"It is time Julie," replied the Master, "for you to make decisions about the next phase. From your life, you must now select three events that, if you had the opportunity, you would change. Take your time and choose wisely. This is not as simple as it sounds. These events must show the learning you have acquired. How you change them must be closer to the higher law and display what you have learned.

"Your selection will, in part, influence the next phase in your journey. When faced with this, some have chosen to call it a test. We, who oversee the process, view the selection as evidence of spiritual growth and stretching. All of the capacities taught in this place are inherent in each soul and, as circumstances come together, the higher capacities extend themselves. It is natural, Julie, so do not worry about your choices. What is it that you would like to do?"

Julie thought for a moment and questioned. "If I do not accept this opportunity now, or fail the test, what happens?"

"Nothing Julie. You stay where you are, which in our classroom, until you are ready to choose again. Here, there is no punishment or failure; it is a matter of learning and growth of the soul."

Julie thought for a moment before replying, "You can come in; I am ready for the next step."

"Good, Julie," replied the Master of Light. "However, I do not need to come in. This is something you will do on your own. You will search your own memory and create the opportunity. You will go back into your life and relive the moments. You will recreate the opportunities you missed."

With that, the Master was gone.

Julie was back in his easy chair, considering the task before him. In his mind, he could now recreate his life and relive it. According to the Master, relive it as if it were real. Present before him was the opportunity to redo and correct things that had fallen short.

Julie smiled to himself and thought about some of the sensual experiences he could relive. He could relive nights of excess in his youth. There were experiences with some of the town women where he had fallen short and it might be fun to redo them.

And Julie remembered what the Master said, these were to be experiences where Julie missed the mark and fallen short of the higher call; not moments of failed adventure. These experiences were to represent, while being on this side, those things he had learned. In this effort, choice would influence future decisions and throughout his life, Julie had suffered the long-term effect of making poor decisions; he did not want to repeat this pattern.

As Julie went deeper into himself and focused on the Light, he found himself seated on a park bench. It was a cool, fall morning and the sun was slowly burning off the dew. Reba was seated beside him and she was crying. As Julie focused harder, he could hear her words through occasional sobs. "Julie, Julie, it is always what you want.

Like a little boy you must have your way. Never do you consider how it will hurt me or the children."

Gradually, Julie remembered that morning. It was the day when Reba found out about him and Mrs. Cohen; she had been one of many. Julie could not control that part of his anatomy and it was only biology that slowed him down.

Reba continued, "Don't you have anything to say? Are you going to sit there and say nothing? Or are you going to get up and walk away like you always do?" Julie did not respond, so Reba continued. "Julie, when are you going to grow up and accept responsibility for who you are? You have a family. You have a wife and have made a promise before God. Say something . . . Say something . . ."

When this actually happened, Julie just sat there without saying a word. He said nothing to defend himself or comfort Reba. At the time, he was too ashamed and wanted the whole thing to just go away. On his own, he knew that he could not stop and control himself. God had helped with the impotency.

At the time, he felt badly for Reba and regretted the deep hurt he caused. Yet, he said and did nothing. Here was the opportunity to make things right.

Slowly, in his mind that now seemed as real as anything he had ever experienced, Julie softly spoke to Reba. "Reba, I have been a fool my entire life. Always I have been my own worst enemy, destroying and hurting the things and people I love. Throughout it all, you have been my best friend and I am sorry that I hurt you. You have been the best of wives and I have been amongst the worst of husbands. I am sorry Reba."

Still sobbing Reba looked directly at Julie and replied. "At least you said something this time Julie, you did not get up and run away or sit there like a small, embarrassed boy like you usually do. You have hurt me deeply and I do not know if I can ever forget or forgive this."

For the first time in his life, Julie felt Reba's pain and tears came to his eyes. With difficulty Julie continued, "Reba, without you I would have been even a greater failure. All my life I have ruined things. You and the children are the only good things that have happened to me. Our family and our apartment I owe to your hard work, not mine. I promise I will never hurt you like this again and will try to consider your needs before my own. Can you ever forgive me?"

Reba looked at Julie and said through her sobbing, "I don't know Julie. I just don't know . . ."

Julie found himself back in his easy chair. He thought about that day with Reba and their conversation. This time it was different; Julie had done the right thing.

Originally, Reba said it would be difficult to forgive him, but in time she had. Reba was such a good woman. The part that changed was Julie's response; this time, Julie tried to give something to Reba. He tried to mend the hurt he caused. Julie thought about Reba's need, not his own desire. Thinking of another, considering their need, is the higher law.

Julie was standing and looking out the kitchen window. In his mind, he saw the activity on Union Avenue. He pictured the children playing in the vacant lot across the road – the women sitting on the tenement stoop and talking in front of the building, the shoemaker's shop and the candy store, where the children went after playing and the men discussed politics, sports, and women. All these things seemed real, yet Julie knew they were creations of mind; memories that he stored.

Being dead had certain advantages and freedoms. Basically, you could go anyplace you wanted in your mind and memory. It was a realm you created and, since you no longer had a body, there was no physical pain. Similarly, if you chose to create physical pleasure you could, but it wasn't real and was missing the depth of sensation. However, you could experience the emotional and psychic portion. All was in your mind and memory… and this bothered Julie.

He was in this place, wherever it was, and could think of anything he wanted or desired. All was a thought image but to what purpose? Then, Julie remembered… he was here to go over his life, judge the outcome, and decide the direction he would next travel.

While Julie was free to think and do in his mind whatever he chose, still, there were boundaries and limitations that he could not understand. Without warning, the Being of Light took him places and forced encounters that Julie had to examine. Why certain things took place and who determined what they should be, Julie was unsure and while there was some unease and tension, for the most part this place, wherever it was, felt like home. Julie felt an underlying peace and tranquility. The Light that danced about him was the Light of God. Here there was no need for prayer or repeating the name of God, since everything radiated with beauty, Light and holiness. So, whatever the outcome of this process, Julie was not afraid and knew that God was watching and helping.

As Julie continued to look out the kitchen window, he heard the front door to the apartment open. Turning, he saw Larry, his son, coming into the kitchen. Larry was dressed in a white T-shirt and brown shorts; he looked like he did during the summer of his 18th birthday, right after he graduated from high school.

Walking into the kitchen, Larry greeted his father, "Hi Pop, how are you?"

As was his way, Julie replied, "I'm fine son, how are you?"

"Real good Pop, but kind of upset."

"Why is that, son?"

"Well, you know I was planning to go to Brooklyn College in the fall and become a math teacher?"

"Yes, I know."

"Now Mom doesn't think that is a good idea. She says she needs me to go to work and make money. She says she can't keep things going by herself. You rarely work and now that Laura and Judith have their own family, Mom needs me to help out around here. I know she needs help with the bills, but I really want to be a math teacher. I don't want to disobey Mom, but what do you think?"

Pausing in his mind, Julie remembered that day as if it were yesterday. It was nearly 30 years ago and Julie was still ashamed about his answer.

Larry went out to work and never became a math teacher. In a way, Reba was right; they did need the money. Julie could not support the family and find the "right job."

Being a Kohen, son of a Rabbi and in the line of priests, Julie felt manual labor was beneath him. As a youth, he refused training in a profession and fell upon tailoring by chance. Most Jewish immigrants found work in the garment district; it was the only work available and Julie's heart was never in it. Not being a very good tailor, he was lucky to work two months a year.

Reba was the hard worker and did whatever was necessary. Even when they became superintendents of the new tenement building on Freemont Street, it was Reba who took out the garbage cans to the curb and it was Reba that learned how to fix leaking faucets and toilets.

As Julie watched Larry grow older and raise his own family, he saw Larry repeat some of Julie's mistakes. Larry went to work that summer, then entered the Navy, then married. Larry never took the time to be trained in a profession he felt proud to be part of. This failure, in many ways, was Julie's failure as well. Julie never encouraged his son to follow his dreams, to go to college, to become a teacher. Who knows how Larry's life might have changed, might have been easier. Larry worked so hard.

At the time, Julie selfishly realized that if Larry didn't help with the bills, then Julie might have to do something. Reba was right; they did need money, though it was not until years later that they moved into the less expensive, subsidized housing.

Julie and Larry were now back at that same place, 30 years ago. This time Julie would help his son and offer guidance and support.

"Larry, my son, go to Brooklyn College and become a math teacher. You don't have to go to work or worry about money for your schoolbooks. I will tell Reba this is my decision. Somehow, I will find work and do whatever it takes so your life will be a little easier. You need to be trained in a profession, so you will not struggle to take care of yourself and family.

"Your mother is right, someone needs to work and help out, but it should be me, and not you."

Then, Julie and Larry drew closer and embraced. And with this embrace, Julie shattered the cycle of pride and stubbornness that controlled his life. He gave up part of himself and promised to work as a laborer so his family could eat and his son could have the opportunity Julie turned down.

What good is experience if you do not learn from it? What good is wisdom if it is not put to work in the world?

Julie wiped the tears from his eyes and thought, if he only could have done this while he was alive. Did it really matter that he had done the right thing now? What was the connection between this place and his life in Brooklyn?

Julie remembered the teaching of the Being of Light, "All things are connected in the Light and with God. With all thoughts and actions there is energy. When this energy is connected to the greater good, everyone benefits."

Julie knew he had done a good thing; where it would lead, he did not know.

Suddenly, Julie found himself in the small Shul on Union Avenue. He was in Rabbi Simon's office, waiting for the Rabbi.

Julie wondered what he was doing here. What unfinished business did he have with the Rabbi? They had been such close friends. Then it hit him . . . He knew what he had to say to the Rabbi and why his higher soul had called him here.

Rabbi Simon opened the door and came into the office. He was a busy man and often it was difficult to get a few minutes alone with him. Their congregation was a poor one and the Rabbi was paid a small salary. In addition to his duties at the Shul, to make ends meet, the Rabbi ran an appetizing store with his brother. In this way, Rabbi Simon led their congregation for nearly 20 years.

The Rabbi took his seat behind the desk and said, "So Julie, what is it that is on your mind? By the way, how is your grandson? That was a beautiful Bar Mitzvah service we had. It is so rare to have one during the middle of the week."

"Rabbi, he is doing well and thank you again for your help. But that is not what I wanted to speak to you about."

"What's on your mind Julie? I can see that you are troubled by something."

"Yes . . . I'm deeply troubled and need to speak . . ."

"Take your time Julie, there is no rush."

Slowly, Julie began. "Rabbi, I think it is wrong how we separate the women from the men in our service. The curtain, or veil, between them and God is something men made up to feel superior.

"In my family, Reba has been the stronger one; the one who has lead by example and the one who has lived closer to the higher law."

Rabbi Simon sat quietly looking at Julie and replied, "Continue, I see you have more to say."

"Yes, Rabbi I know that this is our tradition, but to refer to women as the weaker vessel and not allow them to partake fully in the service is wrong. It divides us. In God's eyes, one is not better than another. To the Father, all the children are special; this way of doing things is wrong.

"In my life, I was the one who veiled myself from God. I was the one who set up a curtain between my higher nature and myself. I was too good to labor like other men. Because I was special, a Kohen, I told myself God would forgive my faults. Always, I had reasons not to do the right thing and I can sit before the Torah and partake fully in the service.

"There is something wrong when someone like Reba, who is better and closer to what God wants, cannot sit directly in front of the Torah and I can. Oh, I am so ashamed."

Rabbi Simon looked at Julie and softly said, "I can see that you are troubled by many things. You are confusing aspects of your personal life with the traditions of our people. To me, Julie, this is your personal view. Because you feel unworthy to sit before the Torah, the tradition of women sitting behind the veil is wrong. How are these two things connected?"

"Rabbi, I feel it is wrong that Reba is veiled from the Torah and I am not. Of the two, I am the weaker vessel. Reba has been the stronger one and if only one can have this place, Reba deserves the honor. All of this has made me realize God does not want the veil; this is something men have made up.

"God forgives and loves us. God wants us all to have the place of honor; we are all his children and he loves us, even with our weakness. Reba has taught me that if she can still love me with all my faults, then God, who is infinitely more merciful, wants us to treat each other with love and kindness.

"This curtain and separating the women from the men, is wrong; I know it."

"Julie, this is our tradition; I am only a Rabbi, what would you have me do? Tear down our tradition because you feel ashamed before the Torah and God? Surely you are upset and confusing one thing with another."

"No, Rabbi, I did not come here to have you tear down the curtain between women and God. God never put up the curtain. Men put up the curtain so that we could feel superior to women. Goodness and the ability to live according to the higher law is in everyone's heart.

"God wants us to live a good life and work toward the higher law. I cannot worship here anymore. To me, the curtain represents the veil I have created between myself and God. Also, it represents how I have not lived according to my own higher nature and been true to my wife. Rabbi, you will not see me anymore in this Shul. I will worship in my own heart and try to live a better life."

Julie got up and walked out of the Rabbi's office, never to return.

VI - The Judgment

Julie found himself seated in a meditative position, on a platform, suspended in the air. Across from Julie, to his right, was the Being of Light, who was also in a meditative posture. All about the platform was a fine, gray mist and Julie could not see what lay beyond the platform. Looking up, he saw a beam of Light descend through the mist and land on the platform. This staircase of Light remained touching the platform to the left of Julie. Overall, the surroundings were peaceful and Julie felt calm and at ease.

Again, Julie closed his eyes and felt the Light as it was directed from the Being of Light. Slowly, Julie became one with this Light as it enveloped and caressed his spiritual center. The Light passed from the Source to the Guardians who reflected it to the Being of Light. In turn, it was reflected upon Julie's heart. Julie stayed in this place of one-ness for what seemed an eternity. Here, when one is with the Source, time stands still; there is no beginning and there is no end. All things are connected through this Light and the interplay is love and joy and one-ness.

As the universe continued to travel through the cosmos, Julie, the Being of Light, the stairway through the clouds, and the platform were one. In this one-ness, Julie was home; he was sipping on the meaning of life and the nature of the soul's journey through the many worlds.

In this place of splendor and love, Julie experienced the meaning of life, death, and the connection of his life to all things. Here, in this timeless place, Julie knew the answer to all his questions and cure for all his pain; everything bespoke the Name of the Source.

All of this – the many worlds, the countless journeys – are created to sing the praise of the Source. Man, as representative of the Source, has the capacity to create and destroy. The enabling element, the element of grace that holds all this together, is the Light. The Light is the loving, creative, nurturing energy of the Source itself. Each person, each soul is part of the original Plan; the Plan that holds the universe together and guides it upward. Each soul is created to travel through the different worlds, making each better until the moment when the soul arrives back home, completely one with the Source.

The point of each life is to know this and become one with this. With this spiritual knowledge of what is to be done comes the responsibility and capacity to serve. Each is created as an extension of the Source, so they can rise up in their spiritual glory and serve the Source. This is the point of the journey; this is the point of the many worlds.

Julie continued to drink in this knowledge and wisdom, staying in this loving place, feeling the Light within himself begin to stir. As the Being of Light continued to reflect the Light upon Julie's heart, Julie felt the change within and became his own light for the dark night. He was aglow with the Light of eternity; Julie was finally home.

In time, when Julie opened his eyes, he turned to the Being of Light and they communicated through the Light. This communication was spiritual, without words, mind to mind.

Julie said, "I am ready."

The Being of Light replied, "So, what have you learned?"

Julie responded, "Each soul was created to go out into the universe and serve. In its travel through the many worlds, the soul is destined to grow strong in one-ness with the Light. The point of the journey is to join the Light in service, in kingship.

"To assist in this effort, a ladder, or stairway, was created. This is the Path of One-ness and has existed since the beginning. It is the way of service, Light and knowledge. It has no name but has an existence. This ladder ensures that the Plan is fulfilled for each soul and for humanity.

"This Path of Light is the enriching and enabling element and is linked to the heart of each soul; it is the center. The Source has extended part of itself into this world and into each soul, to ensure that the cosmic dream can become real.

"The point of each life is to grow closer to this reality. The world was created with many beautiful things and potentials. Man is the coming together of flesh and spirit so that spiritual kingship might again shine upon the physical world. Each soul has the capacity to bring part of the Source into the world. That is the dream we call life; that is the potential, the riddle hidden in each. Each can become the creator of a beautiful world, just as the Source is the Creator of the many worlds. We stray from our basic nature when we deny this capacity and do not act in accordance with our higher nature and potential. Each is a child of the Light and has the capability of bringing Light to the darkness. First, we do this within ourselves and then we do it in the world."

The Being of Light continued, "Now speak of Julie and what he learned."

Julie answered, "I came into the physical world to learn, work and serve. I took the physical form so that I might experience the many parts of this reality. The choice between darkness and Light was mine.

"In my many travels through the physical world, I experienced pleasure, pain, doubt, and love. These were gifts to me, yet I did not realize it. I saw some of these experiences as struggles and sought to ease my pain. I ran away from my basic nature and cut myself off from the Inner Light. If I had used these trials to turn inward and unite with the Light, I would have remained true to the original plan. In this failing, that was repeated many times, I lost numerous opportunities to join with my higher nature and make the world a better place.

"Yet, there were times when I loved and held true to the higher law. I cannot dwell in the place of failure, for it was part of the Plan. Each is created weak so that they might turn to that which is strong; the Inner Light. Oh, that I had celebrated more of my opportunities, laughed longer in the sunlight, and frequently caressed those I loved.

"As a child of the Light, I have learned that the capacity to counter the darkness is within each. That is the point of the struggle; that is the point of the journey. Each has within a magic wand to create a world of Light and love. Like the Source, we are creators of both darkness and Light and must use this ability to accomplish higher things.

"If we do not learn this in the physical world, then we learn this in the next world. That is the point of the life; we are creators of darkness and light and, with each decision, grow closer or farther away from our higher destiny."

The Being of Light said to Julie, "Speak now of your judgment. Were you true to your own higher call or did you fall short in your life?"

Julie smiled to himself and answered, "And the Lord said, from one small act of kindness long forgotten shall your soul be saved. If you take one small step toward me I will take ten steps toward you."

Gradually, Julie felt his soul become all aglow and radiate with a glowing intensity. Julie's Inner Light shown brighter and brighter and he felt himself begin to slowly rise, reaching out toward the Being of Light. Slowly, the Being of Light began to move toward Julie. Gradually, the two joined and became one.

And, as the spark became a flame, the entity that was Julie joined his own higher potential and soul. For the Being of Light was, in fact, the capacity that resided in Julie all along, and that which used to be, became that which could be.

And as this unified Light, which was Julie, grew brighter and brighter, it began to move toward the staircase and ascend to an even higher existence.

For, you see, there are many worlds to travel and many worlds in which to serve. This place, this world, is one step along the way back home to our Source.

About the Author

Dr. Stewart Bitkoff, while studying in university, was accepted into another far more mysterious form of learning. While both educational experiences were located in New York City, one specifically trained scholars while the other prepared spiritual travelers.

For 30 years, Dr. Bitkoff has walked the way of the Sufi and reveals in this trilogy ancient mystery teachings in clear and accessible language.

Dr. Bitkoff is the author of multiple titles under the banner of **Goldpath**. After receiving his Doctorate of Education at New York University, he taught in various colleges and universities. Professionally, Dr. Bitkoff has helped the mentally ill integrate their altered state of consciousness into the physical world.